IN OVER HIS HEAD

THE BRIDES OF PURPLE HEART RANCH BOOK 6

SHANAE JOHNSON

THOSE JOHNSON GIRLS

My favorite type of love stories are the ones when one or both of the love interests have a wound, be it internal or external. I love reading, watching, listening to how these two people will work out their differences and, most importantly, heal together. That's what's in store for anyone who visits the fictional Purple Heart Ranch; a place where Wounded Warriors find rehabilitation for their bodies and everlasting love to heal their hearts.

In order to make this particular story, work I had to take some liberties with how things work in the real world, particularly when it comes to the military. When you turn the page, you'll find out that the hero is headed to a bereavement visit. It is not protocol for enlisted men to make bereavement calls before someone who is trained to do so visits the family. I know that. However, leaving out the Bereavement Officer made the story work better. I hope you can suspend your disbelief on that front.

The stories in this series will deal with elements of Post Traumatic Stress Disorder (PTSD). These love stories will presume that love is the key to healing these internal wounds. I know that love is often not enough in matters of this disorder. If you, or someone you love, is suffering from this heartbreaking ailment, please know there is help in the real world. That real world help is often the best form of medicine, along with a side dose of a few sweet kisses.

Love,
    Shanae

It was the metallic smell of fresh blood that knocked him off his feet, not the blast from the bomb exploding behind him. Corporal Brandon Lucas got down, ducking and covering to avoid the deadly fragments that radiated from the center of the attack. From his training, he knew that most of the damage from an explosion was caused in the first few seconds of the blast wave. It was the shock that left a lasting impact.

Heat licked up his back. Screams pierced his ears. Even with his eyes closed, he saw the flames flicker on the inside of his eyelids. When the worst of it was over, he looked over his shoulder. But all he could see was black smoke and orange flames.

There was no one left standing. Not his

commanding officer. Not the other two men on his team. That's when he lost his footing.

He'd been on his knees. As he tried to stand, the combination of smoke and blood knocked him onto his chest. Brandon went down hard.

His palms scraped the coarse desert sand. Dirt mixed with the metallic blood on his tongue constricting his throat. He couldn't speak, but he had to. There were orders to be followed. He was trained for this, though the simulations and drills never quite prepared any soldier for the realities of combat.

He inhaled. Blood wasn't the only chemical smell. Mixed with the synthetic smell of the explosive material were the charcoal scent of gunpowder, the rancid odor of burned flesh, and the toxic fumes of diesel fuels. He knew he had to push past the assault on his nose. It was a rookie mistake, and he was a seasoned officer. The unexpected smells of war typically startled privates who'd just gotten a bit of hair on their chests and dust on their polished boots.

Under orders, Brandon had given the command to proceed. Yet, when he had, there had been hesitation in his voice. Brandon never hesitated. Not once in his years in the United States Army. But something had been off. His gut had told him so. But orders were orders. And so he'd given them. Unfortunately, his team had heard his doubt, and they too had hesitated.

Then everything blew up in their faces. All that was left was blood, and burning flesh, and a blaze. And it was all his fault.

"Lucas, wake up."

Brandon jerked awake at the sound of his superior's voice. He'd only closed his eyes for a few moments. He knew that because the last time he looked at his watch it had been five minutes ago. But that was all it took for the scene to invade his dreams and assault his senses like he was back in that village with smoke and gunfire and the cries of women and children and enemies all around him.

That was not the scene before him now. The sun was peaking up past the horizon. He'd watched it go down the previous night and rise up as it brought forth a new day. The scenery outside the window moved slowly past him as the airplane made its slow taxi to the gate.

"We're here."

Sergeant Colin Chase looked back at Brandon from his seat. Beside him, Brandon felt an elbow from his seat companion. Private Mark Ortega had already unbuckled his belt and was ready to bounce out of his seat. Brandon knew that Ortega was more ready to get out of the confines of their metal transport than he was ready to carry out their latest orders. Brandon saw no reason to rush for that very reason. Also because he knew they had ample time to make their connecting flight.

"Ladies and gentlemen," said the pilot's voice from the overhead speakers. "Please allow our members of the United States Army to depart the plane first. We thank you for your service."

The three men in uniform rose slowly from their seats. Applause sounded from the back rows of the commercial airplane. Chase turned to the civilians at the back of the plane. He put on that thousand-watt smile that had been captured once or twice in military brochures. Brandon swore he heard a few feminine sighs of approval as Sgt. Chase saluted and waved.

Those sighs doubled when Private Ortega, now free from the confines of the window seat, smiled his dimpled grin from the aisle. There was a reason he was nicknamed Lady Killer back on the base. It had nothing to do with his sharp aim and everything to do with those twin bullets on the sides of his face.

For his part, Brandon gave a quick salute and

turned away. He didn't want the praise, not today. Maybe not ever again. His gaze fell on the empty seat beside the one Chase had vacated. Brandon's mind went to the missing fourth member of their team.

"Hey." Chase's hand came down on his shoulder, a vise grip that Brandon knew he'd never escape. "It's not your fault. You did everything you could. We all did."

Brandon didn't nod his agreement. He turned from the empty seat. Reaching up to the overhead compartment, he grabbed his duffle bag and headed to the exit. His movements decisive now that he was back on his home turf.

It was his first time back in the United States in over a year. The heat of Atlanta felt like the same heat he'd confronted every day in the deserts of Afghanistan. Brandon wasn't from Atlanta. None of the men were. This was just a layover. Their final destination was the northwestern state of Montana.

After a favor pulled by Chase, their fire team was headed for some rehabilitation at a ranch run by vets. The Purple Heart Ranch it was called. There, the three remaining members of the team might heal from the ravages of their last assignment. Though Brandon doubted it.

All scrapes, burns, and bruises from the ambush

had healed. Brandon's skin had reknit from the burns. His aches had dulled. It was only his mind that still had an open wound.

They all had open wounds on the inside. Classic symptoms of Post Traumatic Stress Disorder. Brandon's symptoms robbed him of sleep where every time he closed his eyes he'd relive the events of their last mission and his one mistake that had knocked their four-man fire team down to three.

It was supposed to be their last job before their separation from the army. He hadn't expected that separation to be so permanent. But it's what they all had signed up for.

Now they had one mission left before the separation was complete. In this final assignment, they had to tell the family of Private Reece Cartwright that the vibrant young man wasn't coming home again.

At the arrivals gate, people waved signs and held up posters thanking the soldiers for their service. Chase and Ortega put their winning grins on. Brandon forced a smile, but a glimpse in the glass window told him it did not meet muster. Still, he did what he was trained to do, he soldiered on.

CHAPTER TWO

The choir director's fingers struck the first chord on the ancient organ in the church's music room. Voices rose in praise and perfect harmony. It was a joyful noise.

Reegan Cartwright raised her voice alongside the small but devoted choir. This was her favorite song of the program. She closed her eyes as the words of the song penetrated her heart.

There was nothing like the sounds of the choir singing praises on a Sunday. This wasn't a Sunday. It was a Saturday night at choir practice. By the way practice was going, it was going to be a rapturous service come tomorrow.

As the music swelled, so did the passion in Reegan's heart. It lifted her voice. Unfortunately, the note was an octave out of step with the other singers around her. The organ music came to a crashing halt.

Everyone turned to Reegan since the dissonant note had come from her lips. Reegan pressed a hand to her throat, rubbing at the corded skin she found there. This was the third time that day where she'd hit the wrong note on a song she'd sang in perfect accord her whole life.

"Is everything okay, Reegan?" Barbara Bowen, the choir director, asked her. "Are you coming down with something?"

Reegan checked in with her body. She did feel out of sorts, but not the yucky feeling that accompanied a cold. She pressed the back of her hand to her forehead and was met with cool skin. She swallowed a couple of times, but there was no scratchiness in her throat.

"I'm fine," she said. But even those words hadn't felt quite right. "I'm just going to grab a drink of water."

Reegan stepped out of the group. Her friends and neighbors that she'd known her whole life all made room for her to take a moment to herself. These were the same people who had rallied around her after she'd lost her parents three years ago. They were the same people that invited her to family dinners every Sunday night or on holiday weekends now that her parents were gone and her brother was away. She loved each and every one of them and couldn't fathom her life outside this community, her extended family.

Her twin brother Reece was off overseas serving his country, just as he'd always dreamed. Reegan was also doing what she'd dreamed of. Singing in a choir was all she ever wanted to do in life.

Her mother had joked that she'd come out of the womb singing. That even when baby Reegan had awoken her late in the night, it had been the most resonant cries she'd ever heard, and she was tempted to listen to Reegan's wails rather than offering her comfort to get her quiet.

The moment she could join, Reegan had signed up for the youth choir. By the time she'd become a teen, she'd graduated into the full choir with the other adults. Reegan spent all of her time singing. But not just any singing. She might hum along to a pop hit or country song. But gospel and hymns were what brought her joy.

Singing in the church that she was raised in, the church her parents were married in, the church she and her twin brother were baptized in, that was the dream. And she was living it. Even though her parents had passed on and her brother was away saving the world in the service, Regan was living her best life.

She sipped from the cool water in the cup. The liquid slid easily down her throat meeting no obstructions or sore spots. When it reached her chest, it met with a rumble there.

Reegan rubbed at her chest. Her palm rested on her heartbeat. The organ raced, beating twice as fast as normal, as though she'd just run down the hall. But she hadn't. So why was her heart racing as though something was wrong?

Reegan took a few deep breaths. And almost instantly, her heart rate settled. She continued breathing deep as she made her way back to the music room. She even practiced some runs. Everything, her pulse, her vocal cords, all seemed to be back in working order.

When she rejoined the group, they tried the song again. This time Reegan hit all the notes with no problem. The song finished, and the choir was once more in perfect harmony. As she packed up to leave, Barbara pulled her aside.

"Do you think you'll be ready for the solo tomorrow?" Barbara asked.

Reegan loved adding her voice to the group's. But she never felt closer to heaven than when she got the spotlight on the stage. "Of course, I will. I think I just may be tired, that's why I missed the note."

"I'd have to agree, Reegan. You're always overextending yourself. If you're not here volunteering at the church, then you're out at someone's house giving them your time. Or you're off at the Purple Heart Ranch working their gardens."

That was Reegan's other passion. She had a small plot of land out back of her house that she and her mother had turned into a small garden. But on the ranch, she had acres she could plant and cultivate. In the last year that the ranch had been open, it had become her second favorite place in the world. The first being the home she'd lived in her whole life.

"I like being busy," she said to Barbara. "And I like giving my time to others. I have the luxury of not having to work since I live rent free and my parents left me a small sum to live off."

Reegan hadn't gone to college or pursued any work other than giving her time to others. She hadn't wanted to waste her parents' money on an overpriced education when she knew singing was her passion. And that the only place she wanted to sing was in her church choir. Plus, her parents' hard earned money had been reserved for her brother who had realized his dream of going into the Army.

To that end, they'd left Reece the house and Reegan a nice monetary sum. Being true twins, the siblings had decided to share their inheritance. They hadn't even needed to speak their decision. Being connected in the way that twins were, they just knew each other's decision.

So, Reegan stayed in the house while Reece went off to save the world. She invested a good portion of the money in repairs on the ancient home, though there was a lot more she had to do. But those repairs could wait until the next time Reece came home, which by her calculations should be soon. Her heartbeat sped up again at the thought of having her brother home again.

"I'll go home and get a good night's sleep," Reegan said to Barbara. "I promise I'll be rested and ready in the morning."

CHAPTER THREE

Brandon's eyes were wide open as their connecting flight began its descent. He looked over at Chase's and Ortega's faces in the two connecting seats. Blessedly, they were in three adjoined seats in the middle row this time. The fourth seat was occupied by an elderly woman.

Chase and Ortega had slept through the afternoon flight. Each man's eyes were shut, gripped in the peace of sleep. Ortega's mouth was slightly open, a quiet snore whistling out of his nose. Chase's head was tipped back against the headrest. His jaw a firm line that brooked no nonsense even in repose.

Not too long ago, Brandon had come upon a similar scene. Though back in the desert both men had lain in the dirt with their eyes closed. Their uniforms weren't pristine as they were now. Dirt, dust, and blood had covered them. Instead of the calm and soothing voice of the flight attendant giving landing instructions, screams and groans had sounded in the chaos after the gunfire and ear-wrenching explosion had died down.

Brandon hadn't known if the two were living or dead. He was hurt himself, but he managed to crawl to them. Ortega was closer, and Brandon reached out and found the pulse at the man's limp wrist. Before Brandon could get to Chase, the man was already rising to his feet.

The Terminator, Sergeant Colin Chase had been known as back on the base. His fellow soldiers swore he was more machine than man with how far he could go and his expectations that those behind would keep up. Also for his relentless pursuit of his targets. Their last mission was the first time he'd returned empty handed with no asset and missing one of his own.

When the smoke had cleared, Brandon had wanted to stay behind and at least look for Cartwright's body. But they had been compromised. The last Brandon had seen of the private had been the man headed directly into the line of fire. And then nothing.

It was as though he'd disappeared into thin air. It was possible he'd been taken out by the bomb. Brandon hoped that had been Cartwright's fate. If he'd been captured by insurgents, his end would have been far more gruesome.

Chase's eyes opened. His green eyes focused on Brandon like a heat-seeking missile. That strong jaw hardened into steel making Brandon wonder if he were built out of metal like the machine he was accused of being.

"You good?" asked Chase.

Brandon wasn't. Chase knew that. None of them were, but they didn't talk about it.

"I'm good." Brandon gave a quick nod of his head, not meeting Chase's penetrating gaze.

"Did I just wake up in a chick flick?" Ortega stretched his limbs over his head and arched his back with a loud yawn.

The captain's voice came on overhead, telling the passengers to prepare for landing. It was a smooth landing. Not even a bump as the wheels touched down on the tarmac.

They were there. Their final destination after

three days of traveling first from a military base, and then the long flight across the ocean, and a somewhat shorter flight to the middle of the country.

They were travel weary. They each needed a shower and change of clothes. A hot meal was certainly in order.

All around them, travelers rushed to retrieve their bags and line up in the aisle to be the first off the plane. All three soldiers held their seats. Not one of them was anxious to complete this final mission.

Once the aisle began to clear, Chase took a deep breath and rose first. Ortega followed suit. And finally, Brandon rose to join the rest of his unit.

He'd never gone to a family to deliver a death notification. This wasn't the usual protocol, but Chase had pulled some strings. Reece had served under him since he'd strapped on his first pair of boots. The kid had been like a true younger brother. He'd been about to advance in rank before they'd lost him.

In his career in the United States Army, Brandon had lost people. But there had been more civilians who'd passed than soldiers. Far more deaths had happened back home due to illnesses and accidents than in war zones. Modern warfare was a different beast these days. Still dangerous, but with new tactics, casualties were down.

Private Cartwright should've still been here but for Brandon's hesitation. And now, he'd have to face the man's family and tell them that Reece wasn't coming home. But worse, they had no body to bury.

"There is nothing you could have done," said Chase.

They were alone on the plane now. Brandon's arms were raised in the act of retrieving his duffle, but he hadn't brought his belongings down to him. He'd just stood their frozen, lost in the memories and guilt.

"There is nothing any of us could have done," Chase continued.

Brandon nodded, though he didn't believe the other man's words. Just like they were all fine.

The walk through the terminal was blessedly quiet as the hustle and bustle of the airport whirled around them. Chase's gaze remained alert as his eyes darted here and there. The instinct to look for threats would never leave any of them.

Ortega's dimples were hidden behind a stern look as he gripped his bag with one hand and balled his fist with the other. Sweat threaded his dark brow. Walking in civilian areas were always the hardest. It was always possible that a threat could materialize out of a child or a woman.

Finally, they made it to the glass doors that spilled out into warm Montana sunshine. The landscape had been breathtaking from the air. It reminded Brandon of the beauty of Afghanistan.

The middle eastern land was a beautiful oxymoron. Filled with demanding deserts as well as lush valleys. Tall mountains and stunning cities. It wasn't until driving through the human settlements that the ugly underside was revealed. Bombed historic sights, toppled monuments, and decrepit homes where civilians hid, trying to carve out a semblance of life.

Back on U.S. soil, the buildings he could see from the airport were all intact. Cars made their way down the streets with little to no obstruction. Pedestrians walked without a care.

Standing on a curb, a man held up a sign with all three of their names on it. He didn't wear fatigues. He didn't need to. That he was a soldier was clear in the way he stood and the seriousness of his features.

Chase stuck out his hand. "Good to see you again, Sergeant Banks."

"You too, Sergeant Chase."

The two men clasped hands. Dylan Banks held on a moment longer. Chase took a deep breath and let it out slowly. It was the most emotion Brandon had ever seen the Terminator display.

"You didn't have to come all this way," said Chase after he released his friend's grip.

"It's my honor," said Dylan. "We're all excited to have you at the ranch."

"I'm excited to see what you've built."

Dylan nodded with clear pride. "You'll find a state-of-the-art rehabilitation center. Everything from horseback riding to strengthen injured or missing limbs, gardening to increase the dexterity of injured fingers or improve hand-eye coordination. We even have a therapist. The Purple Heart Ranch treats both external and internal wounds."

Brandon frowned at that. He'd accepted the invitation to stay at the ranch for a short duration of time. More of a decompression time before he made his way back into civilian life if, in fact, that was the route he was going to take. He was still leaning more toward re-enlisting and redeploying.

He couldn't deny he needed a few weeks of R&R. But Chase had said nothing about internal healing. He was fine. They all were.

Ortega looked to have the same sentiment. But both Ortega and Brandon held their tongues out of respect for the men of superior rank. Chase would get an earful later.

"We'll head out now then," said Dylan.

"We do have to make one stop," Brandon spoke up for the first time.

"Oh, don't worry," Dylan chuckled. "There's plenty of food waiting for you."

"No," said Brandon. "We need to notify a family." He didn't need to elaborate.

Dylan's face sobered in understanding. "Here in the city?"

Chase nodded. "Yes, for Reece Cartwright."

Dylan winced.

"You knew him?" asked Chase.

"Not him, his sister. She does volunteer work on the ranch. His parents died three years back before we arrived on the ranch."

Brandon remembered that. Reece had been given leave during their training to mourn his parents. He'd come back hardened, even more dedicated to his job in the service.

"Reegan sings in the choir. In fact, she'll be at church right now. It's best to take you there. I think it will be better for her to be surrounded by those she loves when you deliver this news."

Brandon wasn't so sure. He preferred to suffer in silence, in private. But he didn't argue. It would be fine.

CHAPTER FOUR

On Sunday afternoon people flocked into the church's open doors as though it were an Easter Sunday service. Many of the worshippers lingered in the doorways catching up with their neighbors. They stood in the aisles and bent over pews to gossip or extend well wishes or kiss newborn babies. The conversations weren't overlong as most people had seen each other either the day before or a few days ago. But this was the way of their community, and Reegan reveled in it.

The church members in this congregation were lifelong friends. Everyone knew everyone. People of every age took their seats amongst the pews. Some in their Sunday's best, which might have been a suit and tie or frilly dress and patent leather shoes. Others were donned in the best that they could do, which might be pressed jeans and a collared shirt or a hemmed skirt with a little scuff to their second-hand shoes.

Reegan watched as the senior pastor, Pastor Barrett made his way to the pulpit. The man gave her a secret smile as he always did. Pastor Barrett had been the youth pastor when she was a girl. He had been there for her whole life, and she'd spent a lot of time not only under his wing but in his nest making a mess with his young daughter.

Elsbeth Barrett stood at the doors to the church, greeting the stragglers as they made their way in. The pastor's daughter and Reegan had been best friends from the cradle. They'd shared their toys, their clothes, and their dreams. They'd even shared a best friend between them.

Reece was the third part of their trio. It made sense that because Beth and Reegan got along so well, and Reece was a carbon copy of Reegan but with boy parts, that they should get along too. And they did.

Reece looked at Beth as a second sister. Unfortunately, he never looked at her any other way. Even though somewhere around middle school, Beth's view of her bonus brother had shifted.

Thinking about Reece made her heart pound. Reegan was missing her brother more and more each day. It had been over a month since the last time she'd heard from him.

The twins had always had a connection. Reegan swore she could feel when he was upset or hurt. She didn't feel that now, but she still felt ... off.

They'd gone longer stretches where he couldn't communicate. It didn't make it easier. She knew he'd be home soon for some downtime when his enlistment with the army was up. But she also knew that Reece had every intention of re-enlisting. Service was her brother's passion, and she was a proud Army Sister.

"You good, Reegan?"

Reegan turned to look beside her. Cassie Ramos sat beside her, her hand resting on her belly bump. The slight young woman was more belly than anything else these days.

"I'm fine," said Reegan. "Don't worry. You won't have to step in for me."

Cassie, who had the soprano voice of an angel, had been doing her fair share of solos since joining the choir only six months ago. But her voice had changed during her pregnancy. It would often pitch lower in the middle of a song. It was as though she were going through an adolescent boy's puberty.

"Good, cause this kid is kicking up a storm today," Cassie said. "He's got too much of his daddy in him."

Her husband, another armed forces vet, looked up from his place in the congregation as though he'd heard his wife invoke his name. With their young daughter in his lap, Xavier Ramos kept an ever watchful eye on his wife. Reegan had to look away as a secretive smile crept across his face, causing his dimples to make an appearance.

The doors to the church opened again, letting in the last of the setting sun. Four men came in. The first man she recognized.

Dylan Banks walked smoothly down the aisle. Only someone who knew the man would know that his right leg was a prosthetic one, put in place after he lost his leg in the service. The man strode with easy confidence until he found space for himself and the three soldiers behind him.

The other three men were dressed in the familiar green uniform her brother wore. Their faces were serious. Their postures stiff.

Reegan was certain they had likely just come off

a base where they'd been steeped in training. Or perhaps they'd come from time overseas. They had that look about them that her brother had when he returned home for his short stretches.

As they sat, their bodies were ever alert. Backs straight. Gazes roaming, darting here and there. Sizing up everyone and everything in their periphery for a sign of threat.

It had alarmed Reegan the first time she'd seen her brother react that way to the people he'd known all his life. But he'd explained that hyper-vigilance was a soldier's greatest defense.

All three soldiers had dark hair, but Reegan's gaze caught on the one lagging behind. There was no height difference making him taller or shorter than the other two. His body wasn't broader or leaner than the others either. Though one soldier had striking dimples that rivaled Xavier's, and the other had striking green eyes which had already caught the attention of a few of the single women in the congregation.

Reegan's gaze caught and held on the third soldier precisely because he did not look up. He looked bone-weary tired. The dark circles under his eyes called out to her, begging her to run her thumbs beneath them to clear some of the dusk away. The firm set of his jaw urged her to say something to tickle his funny bone. He looked like he definitely needed a good laugh, but she knew that even a grin would be hard won.

The tap of the microphone brought her attention back to the service. Looking over, Reegan noted the new youth pastor Walter Vance was taking the pulpit. Pastor Vance nodded at Pastor Barrett. The young man of God's enthusiasm at giving his first sermon was hard to miss.

"The reading today is from Genesis 2.18." Pastor Vance waited while everyone found the place in the Bible. "The Lord God said 'it is not good for the man to be alone. I will make a helper suitable for him.'"

Pastor Vance gave a pointed look to Elsbeth who had taken her seat in the front pew. Reegan knew the man was interested in the pastor's daughter. She knew the two had gone on a few dates. But Beth had kept a tight lip on the relationship ... or perhaps it was only a friendship? Reegan wasn't sure of Beth's level of interest in Walter.

"The companionship of women was designed by God," Walter continued. "God made Eve, but that wasn't the end of it. Adam and Eve made sons and they begat sons, who begat sons, who begat sons, who begat ..."

The audience giggled and chuckled as Pastor Vance took a deep inhale to replenish his lungs after all the begetting. Reegan couldn't deny that the man knew his way around a pulpit.

"Until eventually we were all here. We are all made up of different chords of the same music. We are meant to be played together. In our community, in our relationships, we are called to come together in harmony and unity. You're not meant to be alone."

Pastor Vance paused for effect. He repeated that last phrase, pointing to people in the pews for effect.

"We are meant to serve. It is His design. He called for us to come together in harmony and unity with one another and be one. I don't know about you, but that makes my heart sing."

A chorus of *amens* sounded through the hall, rising to the rafters. Reegan chanced a look at the three guests clad in uniform. The green-eyed man smiled politely, but it wasn't clear if the message penetrated. The dimpled soldier nodded his head and mouthed the word, *amen*. But the third soldier, his head stayed bowed. Reegan knew it wasn't in supplication. Though she could no longer see it, she knew he was still looking discreetly at his phone.

With the sermon delivered, the chords of the

piano began. The choir rose. Reegan took her place out front to perform her solo.

She inhaled deeply, asking the butterflies gathered there to settle. She'd sang in this choir, in this very spot, more times than she could count. But something was different about today.

At first, every chorister's voice rose in harmony, just as Pastor Vance had preached. But then accompanying voices died down, leaving Reegan's voice on its own.

Reegan took a deep breath and opened her mouth. She belted out the lyrics only to be slightly off-key. There were a few frowns amongst the congregation. They knew what she was capable of and waited for her to shine.

Her gaze found the soldier still on his phone. She had the misfortune of catching his right eye wince at her blunder.

He lifted his head then. Dark eyes met hers, and she felt as though they penetrated past her heart and into her soul. From somewhere beyond, an angel started to sing. Her voice was lighter than a harp's strings. It had more whimsy than a flute could muster.

The soldier's gaze widened. That firm jaw loosened, and his mouth went slack. He sat up taller, his phone forgotten as the voice continued its joyful noise. His eyes were locked on Reegan as though he'd just seen a wondrous sight. And then Reegan realized; that joyful, angelic sound was coming from her.

Brandon's stomach grumbled as he sat on the uncomfortable wooden bench. People in the pews in front of him turned to look back at him. He shrugged apologetically. What could he say? Church had never agreed with him.

As a kid, he'd tugged at his shirt collar which always had too much starch. He'd scrunched up his toes in the pinching dress shoes which he was never allowed to play in and only wore a couple of times a month. He only ever had to go to church services with his grandma. Mostly on holidays or if his grandma had someone to impress on a given Sunday.

Brandon's parents were happily holiday Christians who only ever went on Easter and

Christmas. They called out to God a lot and not in a prayerful way. Typically, in elaborate, sailor-wincing curses, which Brandon had perfected during his time in the military.

But sitting still in a church? That was not his thing. He'd rather have to sit still in a foxhole.

However, this was his duty. And he'd do it. He owed it to Reece. And so he sat still ... for all of five minutes before pulling out his phone and looking for a distraction.

As always, his mind raced when he was forced to sit still. It went back to that village in Afghanistan. Back to the smoke swallowing Reece whole. Back to the explosion ringing in his ears. Back to the crushing guilt he felt for his moment's hesitation.

What he wouldn't give to take it back. To yank Reece back to him with certainty. Unfortunately, that was one thing in this life he was certain of, you couldn't go back and correct your mistakes. You had to face them and move on.

All around him, the congregation murmured praises and *amens*. Brandon should relax in the comfort of their exaltations. Pretty soon, their gazes would turn on him in despair and disappointment when they learned the news that their favored son was gone.

Brandon knew that Reece Cartwright was a devoted Christian. He carried a worn Bible with him wherever they went and wore a gold cross around his neck alongside his dog tags. He could imagine the young man sitting in the pews listening to the sermon and making notations in his book.

Listening to the young pastor speak, Brandon decided he liked that the man spoke to the congregation and not at them like the gray-haired men that had always lorded over his grandmother's church. However, the sermon wasn't one he felt pertained to him.

Brandon had no intentions of begetting or getting married. He still wasn't entirely sure he wasn't going back into the military. He knew for certain he wasn't cut out for this type of civilian life; one where he'd dress in slacks and narrow-toed shoes and sit on a hard bench for hours each week. And on a Sunday afternoon at that.

No, his life would be of more use in going back into the military. That was how he planned to be of service. That's where he would find his fellowship. That's where all of his relationships were forged. He wasn't suited for a life of musical chords or whatever. He'd find harmony within the ranks, unity within a unit.

He looked down at his phone, scrolling through the openings and re-enlistment data on the army's website. He knew Chase and Ortega were finished with their time in active duty, but Brandon decided then and now that he wasn't. How could he be after his last mission and his failure?

There was an itch to get back out there. To make a difference. He'd never felt more human than when he was in service.

It's just that he was so tired. Likely because he hadn't had a good night's sleep since the explosion. He would take advantage of this downtime. He'd relax at the ranch and try and quell the demons that kept him from sleeping. But make no mistake, he was going back.

His nightmares posed a disadvantage to his fitness to serve but not a big one. What soldier didn't have nightmares about what they'd seen in combat zones? He didn't have suicidal or homicidal thoughts. Just memories and guilt over what could have been, what he should have done.

The chords of an old organ began to play. A shudder went down Brandon's spine. This was truly his least favorite part of a church service. The part where regular folk who often were tone deaf raised their voices in an old, sleep-inducing hymn.

Well, on the bright side, maybe the song would send him off to some much-needed sleep.

At least the organ was in tune. And the lady playing it appeared to have the needed skill to command it. The group of singers wasn't half bad, and the song they sang, though not modern, was at least upbeat enough to keep him awake.

Then the soloist stepped forward and hit a wrong note. Brandon felt the impact of the note land somewhere in his gut. It resonated inside him, like a doorbell ringing in the middle of the night announcing the arrival of someone he wasn't expecting.

Brandon was already irritable from not having slept in over seventy-two hours. He tugged at his collar, feeling lightheaded. His fingertips and toes were numb. His heart rate kicked up. He felt as though he were back in a war zone with rockets flying overhead.

That type of adrenaline was normal in duty. But once in civilian life, where being on high alert wasn't necessary, it was disorienting. And then, like the sun breaking through a cloudy day, a voice rang clear through the cacophony of sound that had just assaulted his ears.

Brandon's heart rate began to slow and settle.

The life returned to his fingers and toes as the blood pumped down to the ends of his extremities. He lifted his head and took a deep, filling breath. His eyes locked onto an angel's.

An angel with flaming red hair, so bright it looked like the most intense rays of the sun. Not just red but with hints of gold and orange. Blue eyes as clear as a cloudless day gazed back at him as pink coated lips moved, ushering words from a slender neck. From those lips came the sweetest melody.

Brandon's entire body relaxed. He felt light, as though he'd gotten a full eight hours of sleep every night for a week. He felt like he could float. In fact, he felt his bottom leave the seat as he stood.

A hand grabbed at him, pulling him back down. Brandon looked over to see Chase eying him quizzically. Still disoriented, Brandon retook his seat, but he didn't tear his gaze away from the songbird.

"That's her," said Chase.

Brandon wanted to tell the man to shut it. He didn't want to miss a note of her song. But he also wanted to know who she was.

"That's Cartwright's sister," Chase clarified.

The song ended. The booming sound of

applause filled Brandon's ears. People got on their feet in praise of the choir and the soloist.

Brandon remained in his seat. Getting up and approaching the songbird was the last thing he wanted to do. He'd have to tell that angel that her brother wasn't coming home, and despite what his superiors and the report said, it was Brandon's fault.

CHAPTER SIX

There were hugs and congratulations as Reegan made her way through the crowd of people she'd known all her life. With the services over, most people were making their way to the banquet hall where a potluck was spread over the tables. Reegan held back, not just for the compliments. She held back because she saw that the soldiers had all remained at the back of the church instead of making their way off to the side door that would lead to the food.

All throughout her song, the stiff-jawed soldier hadn't been able to keep his eyes off her. Reegan had even seen him stand up as though he wanted to come to her during the song. He wasn't looking at her now. His gaze was fixed on the floor as he hung at the back of his group.

She knew because she kept sneaking glances at him. She willed him to lift his head and look at her. She ached for the heat of his gaze to touch her face again.

And if he did look at her, what then? Reegan wasn't sure she could ever date someone in the military. Not with her brother's long absences and infrequent calls.

She and her brother had a special connection. Not just because they were twins but because they were close. It tore at her that she couldn't reach out to him any time she wanted. Especially in the last few years without their parents.

It had been hard being on her own. Even though she was never truly alone. She had a community of people to look after who also insisted on looking after her.

Before her parents had died, they'd assumed Reegan would marry and start a family with her own husband. Her parents were traditional like that. Reegan just hadn't found anyone she'd wanted to marry much less make a home with. So, she'd stayed in the house while her parents were alive and after they'd passed on. She kept it for Reece while he was away. And the money that her parents had left her allowed her to fill her heart's delight which was to sing and help others.

Reegan spotted the soldiers speaking with Pastor Barrett and moving steadily forward. Beside the pastor, she saw Elsbeth. It was a perfect reason to go up and introduce herself to the newcomers.

Reegan took a step forward, only to have coldness shroud her shoulders. The looks on Pastor Barrett and Beth's faces weren't filled with the typical rays of joy they showered on anyone who came into the church's doors. Pastor Barrett looked disheartened. Beth looked pale.

Reality hit Reegan square in her chest. Three soldiers in uniform, sad faces, it could only mean one thing. Someone in the church had died. Someone whose family was at this service. There were only three people in the service. Aside from Reece, there was Arnold Bishop and Shelly Turner.

Reegan's heart broke to know that either Arnold or Shelly had been lost. Inwardly, she mourned for their parents. She'd just seen them make their way to the banquet hall. Perhaps she should go after them and bring them back. But she didn't know which family had suffered the loss.

Before she could take a step toward the doorway,

her steel-jawed soldier looked up. His dark gaze found hers. His chin was steel once more. His gaze haunted.

The others looked to her too. Reegan couldn't fathom why? Before she could think too much, they were around her.

"These men have come to see you, Reegan," said Pastor Barrett.

"They have?" Reegan asked the question of the steel-jawed soldier whose gaze hadn't left hers.

"We should go to my office to talk," said Pastor Barrett.

"Why?" said Reegan.

"Ms. Cartwright," said one of the soldiers. "My name is Sergeant Colin Chase."

Reegan knew that name. "You work with my brother. I remember him telling me about a Sergeant Chase."

The man nodded. He wouldn't want to know some of the things Reece had said about him. They weren't mean or inappropriate. Her brother had a lot of fun stories to share about his four-man fire team.

Reegan counted the men. There were three of them. Ortega was on one man's shirt. Lucas was on another. She knew those names. They were Reece's fire team.

Her heart began to pound out of her chest. She clenched her fingers together in anticipation. She looked behind the men, but there was no red-haired private standing in the doorway.

Where was Reece? This had to be one of those internet videos where he'd pop out and surprise her. She couldn't believe she hadn't sensed him near. The two could never sneak up on one another. They were banned from playing hide and seek together when they were kids. They just had a sixth sense about each other. But Reegan didn't sense her brother.

"I'm afraid we have some bad news," said Sgt. Chase.

Reegan didn't look at him. Her gaze connected with the man who'd held her attention throughout her song; Lucas. Corporal Lucas's eyes looked haunted, not mischievous as though he were in on a surprise for her.

"Why don't you tell us the news here," said Pastor Barrett. "We're all family."

Sgt. Chase nodded.

Reegan's head was spinning. Something wasn't right. Her gaze went again to Lucas, searching for the answers there as though she was sure he had them.

"I'm sorry, Ms. Cartwright-"

"Reegan."

"I'm sorry, Reegan, but Private Reece Cartwright has been declared missing in action."

Reegan let out the breath she hadn't been aware she was holding. Relief flooded her, and she pressed her hand to her heart. "Oh, my gosh, you scared me."

The sergeant's eyes widened at her. So did everyone's. Beth's hand gripped hers as though to offer her support.

Reegan took a deep breath and let out another sigh of relief. "I thought you were going to tell me he was dead."

"Ma'am ..." Sgt. Chase looked uncomfortable. So much so that he looked beside him to Cpl. Lucas.

"Ms. Cartwright," said Cpl. Lucas. His voice was deep, resonant. Like a baritone's.

"Please, call me, Reegan," she said. "We're practically family as we both have to put up with my brother."

Reegan knew she should be feeling worried for her brother, but in the midst of his unit, she knew that all would be well. She knew they would find her brother wherever he went missing and bring him back home.

"Reegan," Cpl. Lucas began again. He spoke

carefully, cautiously. "We can't give you the full details as the mission was classified. But your brother was caught in enemy fire. It was the last we saw of him, and nobody was recovered in the aftermath."

Reegan struggled to understand his words. Cpl. Lucas was telling her something important. Reece wasn't just missing. "You're telling me he's been captured?"

Once again, the men looked to one another as though they were at a loss.

"It's unlikely," said Cpl. Lucas.

"Then where is he?" Reegan asked.

The men looked at each other again. Cpl. Lucas looked as though he were battling an inner demon who wouldn't release his words. Sgt. Chase looked to the other man in warning, his features clearly shouted *hold it together*. But it was clear Cpl. Lucas wouldn't. He turned away from Sgt. Chase and faced Reegan fully.

"It's against protocol to classify someone as deceased when there is no body. But for all intents ... your brother ... is gone."

Cpl. Lucas's words were strangled, hoarse, as though he hadn't used his voice in days. He gave her his full gaze, letting her see into his soul. There was so much pain and guilt and— was that shame there?

Reegan wanted to comfort him. She wanted to pull him inside her arms and sing to him. He was clearly in such pain. But all she could offer was her certainty.

"No," she said. "He's not."

Instead of looking relieved at her words, Cpl. Lucas blinked at her in utter disbelief.

"If he were dead, I'd know it. We have a bond. We're twins. We came into the world together. I'd know if he'd checked out on me."

The hall was silent. Her community was used to the Cartwright twins. But clearly, these men weren't.

Reegan was sure Reece hadn't gone on and on about his connection with his sister on the base. But it was true. Reegan knew Reece's heart was still beating because hers hadn't skipped a beat. She'd felt off for days. And now she knew why.

"You're going back to find him?" She addressed this question to Cpl. Lucas. "Aren't you?"

CHAPTER SEVEN

For the second time since he'd come to stay on the Purple Heart Ranch, it was the sound of nature that woke Brandon up. Not the natural sounds of the base where he'd hear boots on the ground trudging through gravel. Nor the all-too-common sound of weapons being cleaned outside of tents. Or foul language being slung about as freely as *uhs* and *ums* to fill the flub between words.

No, these were the sounds of actual nature. There were birds chirping off in the distance. Dogs barking nearby. Was that a rooster crowing out back? And children giggling in close proximity. There were no children at camp.

Brandon was not in a war zone. He was not on a base. He was on a ranch.

And he'd slept.

All night again.

Well, most of it. Sunday night he'd slept four, nearly five hours. Looking at his watch, he saw that he'd nearly cleared eight hours Monday night. He couldn't remember the last time he'd gotten that much sleep.

And peaceful sleep at that. Instead of screams and the orange-red of an explosion, he'd dreamed of a red-haired angel singing a sweet tune as she floated down from a sunny, blue sky. The sight of Reegan Cartwright standing in the midst of the choir, the sound of her voice filling the cracks and crevices of his chest, had been the last thing he'd thought about before closing his eyes. That memory of her had carried over into his dreams.

Reegan had turned Brandon's unwanted nightmares into fulfilling dreams with just the power of her beautiful voice. Unfortunately, now that it was the bright light of day, the reality of the situation struck home.

Brandon knew the five stages of grief. For most people, when they were told of tragedy, disbelief was their first emotion. That denial would be followed by anger, bargaining, depression, and finally, acceptance. Reegan hadn't believed a word they'd told her about her missing brother. She was stuck in the first stage of grief, believing that Reece was still alive.

Brandon hoped that wasn't true. If by chance Private Cartwright had been captured, he'd be experiencing unbearable torture and certain death. For Reece's own soul, Brandon hoped the young man was safely ensconced with his Maker, leaning over the gates of heaven to hear his sister sing.

Reegan's voice had certainly sent Brandon off to heaven while in church and later when he'd rested his head on his borrowed pillow. But the sound of her song was already fading from his memory. And the sleep-stealing numbness was creeping back into his body.

He wondered if it would be possible to hear her sing again? He wasn't sure he was willing to go back through the church doors, sit on the hard wooden bench, make it through another sermon he didn't believe in, and face her denial of her brother's fate for another sweet note.

He had to admit that the notion was tempting. His body felt languid. His mind was clear. Though he could feel memories of the heat of that day crawling across his toes and pinching at his fingertips. It would be back.

For now, Brandon rose to greet the day. He'd been placed in a two bedroom, ranch-style row house all to himself. Ortega was shown to the connecting house on Brandon's left, while Chase was given the key to the one on his right. In addition to the bedrooms, the homes each sported a full kitchen and dining area, along with a living room.

It was a nice setup. Better than most housing on base. But they'd all been told they could only stay a maximum of three months. Something or other to do with zoning? Brandon hadn't been listening. He hadn't planned to stay that long. As soon as he was cleared, he'd be back on a base overseas where he was needed.

Washing and dressing quickly, Brandon stepped out of the front door and was greeted by a pack of dogs. The dogs didn't bark menacingly at him. They were each curious of him. He was curious of them. They were a scraggly bunch. They looked like a pack of wounded soldiers.

There was a tiny Irish Terrier with a wheelchair attachment. A quiet Chihuahua who was missing his front leg. And a Pug with a face only a mother could love who had patches of skin missing from her back.

"They don't bite."

Brandon looked up to see two pregnant women

ambling down the way. The first was a brunette who Banks had introduced as his wife. Maggie was her name. She had a friendly smile that had put Brandon immediately at ease. There had been something in the woman's gaze that had told him that if he were ever wounded, she would be the one he'd want to turn to.

Beside her, he saw another woman he recognized. The blonde had been in the choir alongside Reegan. She had a pleasant voice, but it had a fullness to it where Reegan's was light and airy. She'd been introduced to him as Cassie, the wife of another soldier on the ranch.

"You missed breakfast," Maggie was saying. "So, we stopped by to bring you a muffin and some berries."

The dogs sat obediently. Each set of eyes on the food being offered to Brandon. So, the mutts weren't the welcome crew. They were hoping for a morsel of Brandon's breakfast. Well, that was too bad. He was far too ravenous to share. And besides, the animals looked well cared for.

"Sgt. Chase and Private Ortega have gone for a ride," Maggie continued. "Dr. Patel is waiting for you in his office when you're ready. It's just over that hill."

"Thank you," Brandon said as he took the offered food. The dogs' gazes now swung to him, tongues lolling out of their mouths.

Maggie snapped her fingers, and the dogs all came to attention like good little soldiers. Before she turned on her heel, she called out to Brandon. "I hope we'll see you for dinner."

Brandon gave a noncommittal waggle of his head. Not a nod but not a shake either. The truth was, he wasn't much interested in being in a crowd right now.

Understanding lit Maggie's brown eyes, but she didn't press. The fact that she hadn't pressed, the realization that she would likely give him space, and that the other soldiers and their wives would likely do the same, made Brandon curious to break bread with them. Maybe he would.

He'd been on base around military wives and families. He'd always enjoyed their company more than being back in civilian life. They understood him more. If he ever were to retire, he'd want to do it in a place like this.

Then he remembered Dylan's words. Every soldier who stayed on the ranch had to be married. That was the zoning edict Brandon had tuned out.

At dinner their first night, Brandon had given a

firm shake of his head at the thought. He'd let everyone know that he would be re-enlisting in a few months, and likely re-deploying if he got the opportunity. He would enjoy his time while he was here. Marriage was not in his cards, especially not if he planned to re-enlist.

Brandon munched on the muffin and made his way over the hill. Having grown up in the city, he wasn't used to seeing trees and mountains as far as the eye could see. He jumped at the sound of a mooing cow. He had to wait until chickens crossed the path he was on.

Once he came to the medical building, things began to look more familiar. He walked down the hall until he saw the psychologist's name on the door. The door was open, and an unassuming, brown-skinned man sat behind a wooden desk.

Dr. Patel rose when he saw Brandon lurking in the doorway. "Corporal Lucas, it's nice to meet you."

Brandon looked down at the thin man with a smile bigger than his face. Patel clearly wasn't no nonsense like the military doctors on the base and at the VA Centers. His eyes looked patient and kind, like he had time.

That still didn't change the fact that the man was a head shrink. Sitting across from him, Brandon didn't feel comfortable under the man's gaze. He sat up straight in the plush chair, ever alert.

"I've already met with your other team members," said Dr. Patel. "I'm so sorry to hear about your loss. It's a loss to our entire community. I knew Reece well. His family were all devoted members of my church."

Brandon could only nod. He had no words to offer the man. He'd already botched any attempt to provide solace for Reece's sister.

"It seems you are all still suffering from the loss."

"It's part of the job," said Brandon. "War is dangerous. Not everyone comes back."

"Yet, when it comes to the living, sometimes they leave parts of themselves behind."

Brandon wanted to frown, but he schooled his features, waiting for the psychologist to make his speech plain.

"Sergeant Chase tells me you're having trouble sleeping."

Brandon chewed at the inside of his lip. But he soon realized that if he thought he'd wait out the doctor, he would lose that particular game of patience. Dr. Patel would be just the type of companion necessary for a stakeout.

"It's a common problem," Brandon said.

"Soldiers are often sleep deprived in our line of work. Just like doctors on call."

"True." Dr. Patel nodded, seeming to consider his words. "But you're not on call any longer."

The doctor had him there.

"However, it seems you slept quite well the last two nights. Maybe there's no problem at all?"

Brandon recalled the reason he'd slept so peacefully. A beautiful songbird whose song he'd likely stolen with the news of her brother's demise. The numbness that had been missing the last two days was now creeping into the palm of his hands and up to his ankles. It would likely rob him of his sleep again by this time tomorrow.

"As you know, this is a rehabilitation ranch. I've set your other team members up on healing jobs specific to their injuries."

Again, Patel eyed him with that assessing gaze. Brandon wondered what duties he would be prescribed while on the ranch? He knew there was horse therapy there. He'd like to mount one of the powerful beasts. He'd even be fine with the physical, monotonous work of mucking out stalls. Anything to help numb his brain and his thoughts.

"While you're here, I'd recommend gardening."

"I beg your pardon?" Surely, Brandon had heard

him wrong. "Do you mean you want me to pull weeds?"

"It's soothing watching something grow, caring for something other than yourself."

Brandon blinked. Gardening? Dr. Patel couldn't be serious?

"You'll find the gardens just over the bridge."

CHAPTER EIGHT

Reegan dug her hands into the fresh soil of the earth and hesitated. She was about to pull up a weed. But then she questioned why she was doing it. Why should she end the plant's life just because it decided to start its life next to something others found to be more pleasing to the eye?

This weed was only guilty of trying to thrive in the best place in the garden. The wild plant had the audacity to sink its roots down in the midst of a group of plants whose seeds had been placed there by human hands. But the weed had found its way there through its own grit and determination. It had as much right to life as the other plants that were tended to and coddled.

Reegan let the weed stay for a second, before pulling it up at the root. If she didn't uproot it, it would take not only one flower's life, but likely a few more around it as it sucked up the meager resources of the plot of land. Sometimes things in nature killed for their own survival.

She took a deep breath, breathing in all the fresh life that was on the ranch. As much as Reegan loved going out and helping the people in her community, she loved coming here and helping tend this garden the most. The yard of her family's house wasn't so big, and she easily managed the flowers her mother had planted there since before Reegan was born. She liked the challenge of the acres of pastures that the Purple Heart Ranch provided.

Here she found solitude in all the acres. Here she could think in the quiet spread of land. Here she could tend to herself as much as she did the plants.

Most of the soldiers who came to the ranch for healing preferred to strengthen their bodies with farm work and ride horses to feel in control of something outside of themselves. Typically, it was only her and Reed out in the gardens. The soldier was within shouting distance today.

Reed preferred to work the plants and gain more dexterity with his prosthetic limb. But more and more when he was out there, he wasn't alone. Most of his time was spent making googly eyes at his wife Sarai to notice what needed to be pulled and what didn't.

For her part, Sarai, a former model, didn't get her hands dirty. She chatted with her husband, spoiling the peace and tranquility that Reegan craved. Outside of the garden, Reegan loved Sarai's chatty nature. Just not when she needed quiet and solitude like today.

The couple was quiet today. Sarai had her hands in the dirt, but she neither pulled at unwanted plants or planted any seedlings. Reed ran his fingers over flowers that needed no tending. Today, instead of making eyes at each other, the Cannons mostly snuck glances at Reegan.

Everyone was treating her as though weeds were springing up around her. People who she had been a source of strength for were all waiting at the ready to pluck away anything they thought threatened her light and sustenance. Everyone was treating her with special care, but she didn't need it. She didn't want it.

No matter how many times or ways they said it, Reegan just couldn't come to believe that her brother was dead. It didn't feel like a fact. And no one could prove it to her. Not when she felt the connection that had been between them while still in the womb beating so strong.

Earlier that morning, Reegan had been on the phone with the Department of Defense. But they didn't give her anything more than the soldiers had. In fact, she knew that Corporal Lucas had given her more than he was supposed to.

Reegan had seen the soldiers ride out on horseback when she'd pulled up. She hadn't seen Brandon Lucas's broad form atop one of the majestic beasts. She wondered where he was. Not that she was looking for him.

"Hey, how are you today?"

Reegan looked up to see Beth making her way to her. Beth was dressed in one of her flowery sundresses. But her friend's features were cloudy and gray. Beth's eyes were red and bleary. Her smile didn't come anywhere near her eyes.

Reegan held out her arms to her best friend. Beth sank down to her knees and brought her arms around Reegan. As the two friends held each other, Reegan saw Reed and Sarai make a quiet departure. It was another thing she loved about this community. They'd let one of their own suffer in silence but never alone.

The problem was that Reegan wasn't suffering.

Sure, she was torn up that her brother was missing. She was gutted that she didn't know where he was or what he was experiencing. But unlike everyone else, she knew with every fiber of her being that Reece's heart still beat. If anyone should know Reece was still alive, she'd thought it would be Beth. But by the woman's silent tears, Reegan saw even their shared best friend didn't believe he was still with them.

"I wrote him a letter over a month ago, and he never responded," said Beth. "I suppose this is why."

Reegan opened her mouth to refute the conclusion of that statement, then closed her lips. She was too weary to dispute what she believed, what she knew.

"You know military mail can be delayed," Reegan said instead. "We both have gotten letters from him dated weeks in the past. Once I got one over a month old."

Beth pulled away, wiping at her face. "I hope he got the letter before ... It was a confession."

Reegan didn't need to ask what kind of confession. Beth had been in love with Reece since she understood what the word meant. For his part, Reece was entirely oblivious.

He'd once promised to marry Beth so that they could all be real brothers and sisters. He'd been six when he'd made that promise. Reegan suspected Beth had never forgotten. She was sure their friend had been holding out hope that he'd make good on that promise someday soon.

But when Reece had chosen a military career instead of the call to the pulpit, Beth had had a wake-up call. She'd only started dating after Reece's first tour, and she realized they'd never be together. Reegan suspected that didn't change how her friend felt in her heart. It was evident in the redness of her eyes.

"I told Reece I loved him, that I always had. When he didn't respond, I took it as a sign to say yes to start dating Walter. And now Walter's asked me to marry him."

"Oh, Beth," Reegan sighed.

"I'm going to say *yes*." Beth sniffled as she spoke about her impending marriage. It wasn't a good sign when a bride to be was in tears over the proposal, especially not when she was crying over another man. "Walter is a good man. I can make him happy. Especially if I'm never going to be with the man I truly love."

Reegan wasn't sure what to say. Part of her wanted to tell Beth to wait, that Reece wasn't truly gone. But another part of her wanted her friend to move on. It was clear that Reece didn't feel the same way about her as she did about him. But Reegan couldn't lie, not to her oldest friend.

"I just don't believe Reece's gone," Reegan said. "I still feel him in my heart."

"I hope to God you're right." Beth took a deep breath. "But if you are, I've still got my answer from him. It was never going to be us. I need to accept that and move on."

Reegan knew she should feel relief at Beth's statement, but she didn't. She wanted her friend to marry for love, not to settle for anything less. And she wanted Reece to be there when Beth did walk down the aisle. He would insist that whatever man won his best friend's hand had also won her heart.

Reegan just needed to get someone to believe her and go back and look for her brother. The sun shifted in the afternoon sky and her gaze flicked over the hill. There a man appeared.

He rose up as though he were walking out of the sun. Corporal Brandon Lucas walked toward them like he was the answer to her prayers.

At that moment, Reegan knew what she needed to do. She needed to make Brandon Lucas see the light. She needed to make him believe so that he would help her recover her brother.

CHAPTER NINE

Brandon looked down at the pick in one hand and shovel in the other. He'd held heavy artillery. He knew how to put together a rifle and take it apart in the dark. His skills with a firearm were deadly accurate.

And yet here he was reduced to a gardener. Sent off to battle weeds. Enlisted to sow seeds of string beans.

He didn't have time for this. He definitely didn't have any patience for it. He'd come to the ranch to relax and recuperate, not to tend and till.

He'd figured he'd at least get to ride the horses. He could see Chase and Ortega in the distance trotting on horseback with a few of the other soldiers in residence. And yet here he was walking away from that excitement to commune with nature.

Wasn't the whole point of this to get him out of his head? Not to leave him alone with his thoughts. He was near to tossing the tools down in the cursed dirt when he spotted a red flame up ahead.

It was her. Reegan. She held the same tools in her hands that he possessed. Her tools were buried in the earth. The flowers around her stretched their wiry limbs up for her attention. But she wasn't looking at the blossoms. Her blue gaze was latched on him.

Her gaze wasn't friendly. Those long lashes swept low as she narrowed her eyes. Her nostrils flared. Her arms crossed over her chest, and her shoulders squared off in determination.

She reminded Brandon of a disgruntled kitten. Part of him wanted to toss her a ball of yarn and watch her play. The other part of him recognized the lioness hidden inside that ball of fur.

For the first time in his life, Brandon contemplated running away from a battle line. Because make no mistake, there was a line drawn in the fertile ground. It ended where the weeds were wilting away, losing a battle to Reegan Cartwright's pruning.

He felt her fingers plucking at him. Sifting the soil of his being to get to the root of him. He held still for her, as though she'd taken one of those gardening sticks used to prop up a vine that couldn't hold its own weight.

Brandon stood tall, the tallest thing in the entire field. The sun's rays touched the top of his head first. But he wasn't interested in the star's light. He felt warmed through just being in Reegan's presence. Even though he knew that he was about to get burned, his feet kept moving closer to the heat source.

"Hello, Ms. Cartwright."

He didn't know if he was still allowed the use of her Christian name. When she didn't correct him or insist that he call her Reegan, he knew the privilege had been revoked.

"How are you today?" He tried for politeness. Anything to get a few words from her, to refresh his memory of the sound of her voice. Perhaps once he heard a few more notes, he'd have that peace he'd felt when she sang wash over him again.

Reegan lifted her chin. She inhaled through her nostrils, her lips still pursed. Brandon held very still. Any second she would give him words.

Her chin dipped. She tugged the left corner of

her lower lip into her mouth. Her gaze bounced from place to place. His face, his shoulders, his chest, and back again.

Finally, she settled on his face. She let go of her lip and opened her mouth. Her lips trembled as the words came out.

"I have questions."

Brandon felt his chest sink. He felt the blazing heat of the desert lick over his shoulders. He felt the hairs on his neck prickle with awareness. Danger, his brain told him. Flee, was the response his body told him.

She had questions? Those were the only three words he didn't want to hear from this woman. He'd expected shouting. It had been two days. He'd felt certain she'd moved from the stage of denial and was at anger, perhaps even bargaining. But it looked as though she were still in denial.

He found himself lowering his body until he was kneeling before her. She let out a little gasp at his supplication. Her features softened. Some of her nerve left her for a moment, and she looked unsure.

Brandon had the urge to pull her into his chest. He wanted to tell her that everything would be all right. But that would be a lie.

Reegan still believed her brother was alive.

Brandon knew it wasn't possible. If there was even the sliver of a chance, he hoped Reece would meet his end soon instead of face any torture at the hands of the insurgents who they'd come up against.

"What happened?" Reegan asked, her voice a shaky whisper.

It was a simple question. It was also the root of Brandon's nightmares. Brandon swallowed a few times, but the lump in his throat wouldn't pass to let him speak.

"The last email I got from him, he seemed fine," she said. "He said he was training for an operation and that he would have to go dark for at least four weeks."

Brandon focused on the sound of Reegan's voice. She wasn't singing, but the timber of it soothed him. Even though she was using her melodic voice to speak his nightmare out loud.

"That was over six weeks ago."

Brandon nodded, meeting her gaze. He sat the shovel and pick down and leaned his elbow on his knee to prop himself up. "We did train. And then we went on an operation in Afghanistan. I can't get into the particulars of the mission. It's-"

"Classified."

Now Brandon bit his lip. Everything in him told

him to tell this woman everything. But he'd been well trained. "I can't tell you where. But I can tell you that it was a counterinsurgency mission. We were trying to help keep the peace for the upcoming elections in the region."

The anti-coalition militias in Afghanistan were intent on disrupting the local and national elections. Having officials elected in a democratic fashion would undermine their authority. The insurgents detested the idea of unification of the country but more so a national government.

"Our team was sent to surveil a particular location which had reports of insurgent activity. We were nearing the end of the operation. Everything had run smoothly. And then ..."

Brandon took a deep breath before continuing. Reegan was staring at him intently. He noticed then that her eyes were the same blue as Reece's. It was like looking at the man, like the last time he'd seen Reece when he'd looked back over his shoulder.

Reegan reached out a hand to him. He'd expected her fingers to be pillow soft. But they weren't. There were calluses on her fingertips. The polish on her nails was chipped, and there was dirt in the nail beds.

There was no anger in her gaze as she looked at

him. No accusation. Her eyes held so much compassion. That's what broke him.

"A group of women entered the perimeter. We weren't sure if they were friend or foe. Your brother spoke the language and asked permission to go down to them. I should've said no. But I hesitated. I wasn't sure."

Brandon expected her to recoil from his admission. She didn't. Her rough fingers squeezed his bicep like she was supporting him, like she was there for him.

He frowned at her. Didn't she understand what he was telling her? It was all his fault.

"I was wrong. I should have told him to hold his position. It was an ambush."

"The women were the insurgents?"

"I don't know. We never found out. We tried to get down to him, but there was an explosion. When the dust cleared, they all were gone."

She released her hold then. Her fingers relaxed their grip on his bicep. But her hand didn't leave him entirely. Her palm rubbed up and down his arm.

She wasn't looking at him anymore. She was looking skyward.

Beside them, Brandon heard a small sob. He'd known they weren't alone, but it was the first time he gave any attention to the pastor's daughter. Elsbeth Barrett covered her mouth with her hand and looked away. Tears streamed down her already red eyes.

Brandon was certain he'd get the same reaction from Reegan. But her jaw was firm, determined. Her gaze was clear. And her hand was still on his arm, offering him the support he should have been giving to her.

"So, you think he was blown up?" Reegan asked. "And that's why there was no body?"

Brandon hesitated. Explosions left traces. A recovery team had been sent in, and they'd come back with nothing. It was more likely that the insurgents had taken the bodies.

"Did you go back and look for him? Did they find his dog tags? What about civilians in the area? Did someone question them?"

"It doesn't work that way."

Brandon took a deep breath. He felt the heat of the desert licking over his neck at the rapid-fire questions. She didn't understand. He'd already said too much.

Her hand finally fell away from him. Brandon was left feeling cold, alone in the bright heat of the

Montana afternoon. There were those blue eyes staring at him. Accusing.

"Well, how does it work?" That beautiful voice rose, shouting at him.

"I did everything I could." He shouted, shooting up to standing. He was on his feet, towering over her.

Reegan looked up at him. Not in fear. In shock, confusion, and hurt. The sob that broke from her tore what was left of Brandon's heart apart.

"I'm sorry," he said. But his voice was so raw, the lump so big, he wasn't sure the words even got out. Shame colored his vision until both women were a blur. He turned on his heel and, for the first time in his life, he ran away.

CHAPTER TEN

For the third time in three nights, Reegan's house was packed. Every neighbor from along her block as well as a couple of streets over was in her living room. There were many tears as friends came to grips with the news. There was much light laughter as remembrances of a young, mischievous Reece were told. There was also more food than she could ever hope to eat in a lifetime on the kitchen table.

This was how her community remembered those who had gone home to heaven. The house had been even more filled when her parents had passed on. Those had been the hardest days of her life, but she'd had Reece at her side then.

There were plenty of people by her side now.

The problem was, Reegan didn't feel as though Reece had passed on. She could still feel him in her heart.

All of the mourning going on in the family room was making her itch. All use of the past tense when anyone spoke of her brother was giving her a headache. What she really wanted was solitude.

"Remember how he loved dinosaurs," said Mrs. Peterman from next door. "I brought him a T-Rex, but he wanted a Brontosaurus."

Reegan nodded. She didn't trust her voice not to ring with irritation or her words to be those of a mourning sister. Because she wasn't in mourning.

She felt numb but not empty. She knew what loss felt like. She knew what it felt like when a loved one's spirit left the earth and traveled on. She'd experienced it before times two. This was not that.

She still felt the link between herself and her brother. But she couldn't explain it to anyone else. No one else got it besides Reece. Her twin never spoke about it, but she knew he'd felt it.

Once when she'd broken her arm at Girl Scouts camp miles away, Reece had cried out in pain at baseball practice. He'd been walking out to left field and no one was on the mound.

Reegan didn't feel any phantom pain now. She

just felt tired, and cold, and lonely. Was that what Reece was feeling wherever he was? She ached that she couldn't reach out and touch him, comfort him.

She needed to find someone to listen to her. That someone wasn't Corporal Brandon Lucas. Behind the anger in his eyes, she'd seen a haunted look. Whatever had happened to Reece, he'd seen it with his own eyes and it tore at him.

Reegan had poked at him, but she didn't feel ashamed. She had no choice. Her brother was alive and someone needed to go and find him.

"I put the casserole in the oven, dear," said Mrs. Russo. The woman owned a diner on the main street and made the best lasagna in the entire state. "I had some trouble with the flame."

"The wire's faulty," said Reegan. "I need to get someone out to take a look. I just keep putting it off."

The house was over a hundred years old. It had been passed down to her father from his father who had taken over from his father. Reegan's dad had been in the process of updating all the wiring when he'd passed on. Reece said he'd handle it when he got some downtime, but that was over a year ago.

She'd expected him home next month for some time off. She had a list of repairs they would tackle together. The wiring was at the top of the list.

"Well, I got it on," said Mrs. Russo. "It just needs to be there for ten minutes and then you can eat up. I know it's your favorite."

"Yes, she needs to eat," said Mrs. Peterman. "She's far too thin."

"You really shouldn't be staying here alone," said Mrs. Cottman. "You should come and stay with us. You know we'd love to have you."

Reegan loved her community, but she loved her independence more. When her parents had passed, her well-meaning neighbors had urged her to move in with them, to date their single sons and nephews. But Reegan loved her home. She had no desire to move or live anywhere else. She did want to get married and have a family of her own. But she hadn't felt that special something with any man in town, and she'd met them all more than once.

The closest thing she'd felt to a spark was with a certain corporal. If she were honest, it was more than a spark. She'd felt her skin go aflame the first time she'd seen Brandon Lucas in the doors of the church. It had stoked higher that afternoon when he'd knelt before her in spite of their disagreement. When he'd gone down on bended knee, Reegan's heart had fluttered, and her first thought was that he was going to propose.

"All right everyone." Beth's voice broke through Reegan's insane thoughts. "Reegan's had a long day. Let's let her get some rest."

Reegan could've kissed her best friend for her intervention. In fact, when everyone had filed out of the front door, she did. Reegan pulled Beth into a tight hug and didn't let go for long moments.

"I can stay," said Beth.

But Reegan shook her head. "I just need some quiet."

With a long sigh and one more squeeze, Beth let Reegan go and filed out the front door. Her walk home was short. The Barretts lived just across the street from the Cartwrights.

Once the door closed behind Beth, Reegan rested her head against the wood frame. She felt bone weary. The house was tidy, bless the old biddies who cleaned up after the guests who'd come to pay their respects. There was nothing for her to do.

Reegan headed up the stairs. She wasn't tired. Instead of going into her room, she went into her brother's old room and flipped on the light switch. The electricity hummed in protest but eventually blinked on.

Everything was the same from the last time he'd

been home. That had been at her parent's funeral. She'd made his bed after he'd left and left the comforter on. It had been winter when the funeral was held. The weather was warm now, but she still hadn't pulled off the familiar blanket.

She went to the shelves on the far side of the room and thumbed through his record collection. Reece preferred vinyl to CDs or digital files. He said he liked the scratch of the needle.

Reegan found what she was looking for and brought the record downstairs into the living room. She flicked the switch to the old turntable. The red ON light blinked a couple of times before going solid. Reegan placed the record on the B side with the instrumentals.

The old song was Reece's favorite. It was a duet. Her brother had a strong baritone to her soprano. They'd always sing this song together.

After the melodic intro came the high part. Reegan sang the words of the familiar tune. She went mute when the tune changed and made way for the lower notes that required a baritone's pitch. It was the silence that brought the tears to her eyes.

The lack of the strong familiar voice left Reegan feeling desolate. She searched her heart, looking for any signs that her brother was no longer of this earth. All she felt was alone.

Could she be wrong? Could Reece be gone? Could she just be in denial?

When the tune changed and came back around to her part, Reegan opened her eyes. She was facing the front window. Outside, just beyond the bushes, she saw something moving.

It was a big something. Like a man. There were old men and young boys on her street. No grown men. Only Reece.

Reece?

Could that be him?

Reegan raced to the door. She flung it wide open. Only to sag against the frame with disappointment when recognition dawned.

"I'm so sorry," Corporal Lucas said. "I didn't mean to scare you."

He held his hands up, as though trying to make himself look small and unassuming. It didn't work. He was the biggest man she'd ever met in her life.

His face shifted from placation to alarm. He lifted his head, his entire body going on alert. His nose went up into the air, and he inhaled deeply.

"Something's burning."

CHAPTER ELEVEN

Brandon hadn't meant to be a stalker. He'd meant to come and apologize for his behavior earlier that day. He'd said he was sorry before turning and hightailing out of the garden, but he couldn't sit still for the rest of the day. The heat of his memories from the ambush, the cold lick down his spine of the shame, the numbness of the helplessness he felt knocked into him like a missile.

He couldn't shake it. He had to see her. Not just to apologize, but also to hear her voice again. It was the only salve that had worked.

Not keeping silent about it. Not talking to one of the VA doctors or the ranch doctor. Not listening to gospel music of the exact same song she'd sang on streaming sites. None of it.

The only thing he wanted, the only thing he craved was the sound of Reegan's voice. When he thought of her, the tension throughout his body eased up. When he showed up outside her house an hour ago, just the sight of her through the open curtains loosened the grip of the stressors inside him.

He needed to apologize again for the tone he'd taken with her. But he also just wanted to be near her, to be there for her. That scene back on the ranch, all those questions she fired at him, he knew she was going through the bargaining stage. Pretty soon, she'd be at acceptance, but not before grief sank its claws in her and rung tears from her eyes.

Brandon had an insatiable need to be there when it happened. He'd watched through the window like a stalker as she mingled with her neighbors and friends. All throughout the room people were crying or teary-eyed. Everyone except Reegan. She kept that stiff upper lip, much like her brother wore each day Brandon had known the man.

Though he wanted to be with her, the idea of wading through the crowd of people made him itch. Luckily, the house began to empty soon after he arrived, leaving her alone. Before he could take the steps to knock on the door, she'd started to sing.

He'd morphed fully into a creepy stalker, and standing outside her window. Peering inside and peeping in as she sang a haunting tune.

And then, as though she sensed him, she opened her eyes and looked right at him. Brandon felt like a bug on the wall. He held still, certain that if he didn't move, she couldn't see him. But she had, and now she was standing in the doorway.

Her curvy form filled the rectangular doorway. Her red hair flaming behind her, her blue eyes open wide with a look between fear and hope.

"Reece?"

She mouthed the name, her voice barely above a whisper. But Brandon heard it. What came out loud and clear was the disappointment when she realized that he wasn't her brother.

"I'm sorry," Brandon said coming closer. "I didn't mean to scare you. I just ..."

The night wind rushed him from the side. It brought a familiar smell. The noxious smell of burning gas. The foul smell of charred vegetation. The fetid odor of hot metal.

"Something's burning."

He didn't hesitate. He didn't wait to be invited in. He dashed past Reegan and into the house.

He saw the first spark coming from behind the oven door. The pop, crack, and fizzling sounds of electricity forced him to take a step back. When he did, he bumped into the warm flesh of Reegan.

He might have had time to put out the impending fire. He would never know. His first reaction, his only reaction, was to protect Reegan. He pulled her into his arms, putting his body between her and the short-circuiting appliance.

Brandon had heard men and women in the service talk about their partners back home as their other halves. Reegan Cartwright fit perfectly into his chest like they'd been one whole person who had been carved apart at birth. Now that she was in his arms, nothing would tear them apart.

Except maybe the encroaching flames that were licking their way out of the oven.

He picked her up in his arms and raced through the house. They were over the threshold of the front door when the loud bang sounded. The flames worked fast, eating through the kitchen and reaching for the living room.

Whipping out his phone, Brandon dialed 911. After the call disconnected, he felt the flames growing stronger as they made their way into the front of the house. Brandon expected Reegan to fight to get back, to try and get inside and save her belongings. But she hadn't struggled. There was no fight in her as she watched the flames eat at her house.

By now, the neighbors were coming out of the woodwork. People he was sure she'd known her whole life came up to her. Instead of accepting their comfort, Reegan stayed inside Brandon's arms. She rested the side of her head against his chest. The tears he'd expected the first day he met her finally streamed down her face. Her arms were around him, her nails digging into his back.

The firetrucks had arrived as the flames became visible in the second story windows. Brandon cradled Reegan as they sprayed the blaze. By the time the fire was under control, and only the moonlight lit up the night, the downstairs of the home was charred.

All around her, people made offers of sheltering Reegan in their homes. She didn't pay any of them any mind. She clung to Brandon, wordlessly. The only sound was her even breathing as her chest heaved, pushing out silent tears from the corners of her eyes.

He knew she was exhausted. Emotionally as well as physically. He held all her weight. He knew if he let her go, she would dissolve into a puddle. The last thing he wanted was for her to be out of his arms, out of his sight, out of his care.

"Come back to the ranch," Brandon whispered in her ear.

For the first time since she'd stood on her doorstep looking down at him in disappointment, Reegan blinked. Her head tilted back as she looked up at him. There was only a small light in her large blue eyes. It took her a moment to focus, and then she nodded.

Brandon had borrowed one of the ranch's trucks to make the drive back into town. He tucked Reegan into the passenger seat and strapped her in. When he climbed into the driver's seat, he wondered if he should reach for her hand. In the end, she curled away from him and rested her head against the passenger window.

Guilt hit him on the drive. It ratcheted up as the tires ate up the asphalt to lead them back to the ranch. All the while, Reegan was silent. It all must be hitting her now. Her brother's death as well as the loss of her home.

All Brandon wanted to do was give her cover and

shelter as she felt the effects of her losses. He knew better than to offer her any words. For now, all he could give her was silence.

When he pulled up on the ranch, he parked the truck and came around to her side. After opening the door, he unbuckled her from the safety belt. She practically fell into his arms.

Bringing her into his borrowed home, he lay her down in the bed he'd vacated earlier that night. It was the only one made up. He'd find sheets and take the smaller room across the hall.

Pulling the sheets down now, Brandon placed Reegan's small body inside. She made no move to undress, so he pulled off her shoes and then her socks. It was so intimate to see her pink toes on the white cotton bedsheets.

He felt he should look away. Instead, Brandon tucked her under the covers. He prepared to leave her there to her thoughts when she reached for his hand. Her callused fingers felt fragile on his large palm.

"They're all gone," she whispered, her voice cracking as though it were dry from days in the desert.

Brandon didn't answer. He pulled up a chair

from the side of the room. He kept her hand in his and settled down by her side for the night.

It wasn't like he'd get any sleep. He was certain he'd never sleep again. He'd taken not only her brother from her, but now he was responsible for her losing her home.

CHAPTER TWELVE

Reegan woke up in an unfamiliar bed. Unfamiliar sheets. Unfamiliar ceiling fan. Unfamiliar curtains. Unfamiliar view.

The funny thing was she didn't feel out of place. She also didn't feel alone. Somehow, the unfamiliar place felt like home.

She looked to her right and saw why. Corporal Brandon Lucas was fast asleep in a chair beside the unfamiliar bed she was in. His big body in the small chair looked very uncomfortable.

Realization hit her square in her chest. She was in Brandon's bed. He'd brought her here last night after ...

Reegan closed her eyes. She wasn't ready to face that reality. As long as she kept her eyes shut, as long as she kept the sun out, she didn't have to remember what had happened.

"I'm sorry."

His deep voice penetrated the barrier she'd erected. The walls came crumbling down around her. She felt the heat of his gaze on her face. Reegan opened her eyes, and her heart nearly broke.

There were dark circles under Brandon's eyes. The whites of his eyes were red, not the way they would be from crying. The way they would be if he hadn't gotten any sleep.

"You don't sleep well?" she said.

He didn't answer. Instead, he took a deep inhale, his jaw tightening. He rearranged his large form in the small chair. Had he been there all night? Without asking, Reegan knew that he had.

"Nightmares?" she asked.

Now he looked away. Reegan moved the sheet from her body. She pressed her bare feet to the cold floor only to recoil and tuck them back underneath herself. Brandon inhaled sharply, as though he'd felt the attack of the cold as well.

"Reece has them too," she said. "The nightmares."

Brandon's gaze came back to hers. She knew without him saying that he had fixated on the present tense she used when she spoke about her brother. Her home and everything she owned might be gone, but she was even more certain now that Reece wasn't.

She turned to face the dawning sun. Clouds moved lazily in the early morning sky. She marveled that the scene was so peaceful after the destruction she'd witnessed the other night.

She felt the loss of her home. The place she'd felt the safest all her life. The only place she'd known as home all her life.

She felt the loss of her things. She only had the clothes on her back, and they weren't her favorite. They still had the stains from when she'd been gardening the day before.

More importantly, she'd lost all her journals, her favorite books, her CD collection, irreplaceable picture albums of her family. All gone.

The loss hurt. But one thing remained true. She still felt in her soul that her brother's heart was beating.

That's why she wouldn't dissolve into a puddle of nothingness. She'd lost everything. But she hadn't lost it all.

Reece was still out there.

She turned back to Brandon. He leaned forward,

watching her intently, as though he feared she might fall apart at any second. "Why did you say you were sorry?"

He gulped, the bob of his Adam's apple loosened the steel of his jaw. "The fire was my fault."

Reegan turned her body fully to him. She placed her feet on the floor, ignoring the shock of cold that her toes met. "What are you talking about?"

"If I hadn't been acting like a peeping Tom, you wouldn't have been distracted. You wouldn't have burned the food."

The food? And then she remembered; Mrs. Russo's casserole. "That casserole had been in the oven for at least thirty minutes before the fire happened. It wasn't your fault."

Brandon looked doubtful. In fact, he looked as though a ton of guilt were on his shoulders. Not just the fire that had stolen her home from her.

His shoulders looked rock hard as he sat straight. Reegan wanted to knead the worry out of him. How was it she'd lost everything, and all she wanted to do was comfort this man?

Before she could make a move to offer him solace, the doorbell rang. His body went on full alert. His gaze softened when he turned back to her.

"You don't have to see anyone if you don't want to," he said.

She didn't want to. All she wanted to do was sit quietly with him. She had to admit that a large part of her calm at this moment was due to the fact that Corporal Brandon Lucas made her feel safe.

"I'll get rid of them."

When he stepped out of the room, Reegan pulled her socks on but left her shoes off. She looked around the bedroom. She knew the layout of the row houses having been inside a few of them for dinner with the permanent residents of the ranch.

She knew each of the row houses sported two bedrooms. This room looked lived in but only sparsely. She could tell Brandon had claimed it.

His large, khaki, unpacked duffle bag was in the corner. There was a picture on the bed stand. It was of a younger Brandon and an older man and woman she had to assume were his parents. She saw his uniform hanging in the closet. His polished boots below them. He'd been in a plain shirt and jeans that morning. It was what he'd been wearing last night as well.

Reegan's head lifted when she heard raised voices from the main room. She opened the bedroom door and stepped out.

Brandon stood in the front doorway, his arms crossed like he was a great protector. He turned when he saw her. His look was fierce. Reegan pitied whoever was on the other side of the door.

Coming farther into the room, she recognized who stood on the porch. It was Fire Marshal Porter.

Seeing his orange jacket made all the memories of last night come crashing back to her. The fire. Her home in flames. The grim look on Mr. Porter's face was confirmation; she had nothing to go back to.

"It's all gone?" she asked.

Mr. Porter nodded. She'd expected it. She waited for the impact to hit her in her chest. She waited for her legs to give out. She waited for the tears to sting her eyes.

None of that happened. Losing her parents had been far worse. Learning Reece was missing was in second place. The house, it hurt, but at least she could replace some of what was lost there.

"It's just stuff," she said. "I know my parents took out insurance. It will be enough to rebuild the house and replace some of the things that have been lost."

"That's the problem I was explaining to Corporal Lucas," said the fire marshal.

"What problem?" asked Reegan. She looked from Mr. Porter to Brandon.

Brandon was standing in front of her, facing off against the fire marshal as though ready to fight. But that was ridiculous. Nathan Porter was in his fifties. It would be no contest. And what reason would Brandon have to be angry at the man?

"The house is in your brother's name," said Mr. Porter.

Reegan nodded. Reece had gotten the house. She had gotten cash. That was the way it was set up. She just wished she'd put the money into the wiring instead of waiting for her brother to get home for a DIY project. Then she wouldn't be in this mess.

"The problem is that Reece is declared missing and not dead. There's no death certificate. Without the certificate, the insurance company won't play ball. They won't give you the money to rebuild."

CHAPTER THIRTEEN

"I guess I'll have to move to California with my aunt."

Brandon's head shot up at Reegan's words. He sat next to her on the couch in the small living room. Her hand was in his. He wasn't sure when that had happened, but he did nothing to discourage her strong hold on him.

The fire marshal had long gone, but the news he'd delivered still singed the air. Reegan's house would be declared a total loss. The fire had destroyed the kitchen and severely damaged the living room. The integrity of the upstairs was in question, not to mention that the wiring had proven itself a total fire hazard.

Now, not only had Reegan lost everyone in her

immediate family, she'd lost her home too. It was good that there was still an extended family that she could turn to. Brandon just didn't understand why that family had to be so far away as California?

"You'll stay with us," said Beth.

Elsbeth Barrett and her father sat opposite them. Both Barretts eyed Reegan and Brandon's joined hands. Brandon didn't make a move to let Reegan go. His grip loosened only slightly with Beth's offer.

Brandon wanted Reegan to stay right where she was so he could keep an eye on her. Or hold her hand if necessary. Or wrap her up in his arms when she grew weary.

He knew where the Barretts lived. Their house was in town and not at the edge of the country. If Reegan stayed with the pastor and his daughter, he could at least see her from time to time. Or every day.

Reegan shook her head. "You're getting married soon."

Beth blushed and looked away. Brandon had known a number of soon-to-be brides. He couldn't remember one not beaming with anticipation anytime their impending nuptials were brought up.

"And besides," Reegan continued, seemingly

oblivious to her friend's discomfort, "I can't rain on Pastor Barrett's empty nest dreams."

The older man smiled good-naturedly. "Don't talk such nonsense. You've always been a second daughter to me. You're family, and you're welcome to stay as long as you like."

But Reegan shook her head again, shutting her eyes. "If I did, I'd have to … see it."

She didn't need to clarify what she didn't want to see. When she opened her eyes, she smiled. The smile didn't reach her eyes.

She turned her body to Brandon and squeezed his hand. There was a question in her gaze. Whatever her query was, she was uncertain of the ask. She needn't be. Whatever she wanted Brandon would do whatever it took to give it to her.

"Can I stay here for a while longer?" she asked.

Gasps escaped both Barretts's mouths. Both the pastor and his daughter's gazes widened as though they spotted Beelzebub sitting on Brandon's left shoulder.

"In the spare bedroom of course," Reegan clarified. "Just until I figure things out."

This was far preferable to California. It was even better than her being in town at the Barretts. If she were in the next bedroom, he could watch over her constantly. He could hold her hand. He could hear her sing.

When he didn't answer, Reegan's face fell. "Unless ... of course ... you don't ... I didn't mean ..."

"You can stay as long as you like." Brandon blurted the words out.

Relief touched her blue eyes. Her hold on him relaxed, but he held onto her tighter. He wanted to tug her to him, but he felt certain that would only confirm the presence of a little imp on his shoulder for the others.

"But, Reegan, he's a stranger." The pastor's tone was gentle, but his stern gaze was firmly set on Brandon.

"He was on my brother's team in the service," said Reegan. "Reece trusted him. He put his life in Corporal Lucas's hands. I see no problem with me doing the same, even if only temporary. Besides, you both know the garden is my happy place. I need a little happy in my life after all I've been through this week."

Pastor Barrett looked as though he still wanted to argue the point. Brandon had the urge to ask them to leave. He didn't want Reegan to be challenged, especially if that challenge meant she'd leave his presence.

Luckily, it was Beth who spoke first. "If you think it's best for you?"

Reegan gave her friend a firm nod.

Beth nodded too. "Well, then, all right."

Beth rose and opened her arms to embrace Reegan. When Reegan stood, Brandon found he had trouble unlinking their entwined fingers. In the end, he did let go of her hand. She was staying with him.

"I'll stop by tomorrow," said Beth. "And don't worry, no one's expecting you at choir practice tonight."

"No," said Reegan. "I'll be there. More than anything, I need to sing."

"Okay, why don't you come into town with us."

"I can bring her," said Brandon. The words came out a bit too forceful. He couldn't help it. The idea of Reegan leaving his sight unsettled him.

Beth gave him another glance over beginning at his booted feet and ending at his hairline. Finally, she gave him one last nod. Then after a stern, sixty-second long gaze from Pastor Barrett that made Brandon feel like a naughty schoolboy, they were gone.

When the door closed behind the Barretts, Reegan slumped back down on the couch and into

Brandon's side. He held her, resting his head atop hers. She'd held a brave front these last few days.

Through it all, the news of her brother, her house burning down, she only showed her vulnerability when she was alone with him. Brandon's chest swelled that she trusted him with her worries and woes.

"I'm sorry," she said. "I keep breaking down around you."

"I've got you," he assured her. "No one should have this much put on them."

"I'm sure there's a lesson in here somewhere. Otherwise, what's the point?"

There was no point. Bad things happened for no reason. Or simply because men wanted power.

This woman needed a protector. Brandon had spent his life in service. He was sure he was the man for the job.

"Maybe a change will do me good," Reegan said. "I should probably consider California."

He stiffened beside her. He had to struggle to keep his hold on her light and not tighten like a vise. "But your life is here."

He felt her nod her head against his chest. "This community is my family. But I should probably go and be with my actual blood. Aunt Prudence has been after me to come and visit for two years now, and I've just never found the time."

"A visit wouldn't be so bad." The words were forced from his mouth. Maybe he could make a road trip out of it, and he could drive her there?

"I thought I'd have a family of my own by now and would have been moved out of the house."

A terrible thought went through Brandon's mind. "You're not ... I mean, there's no one ... Are you dating anyone?"

Reegan tilted her head back and looked up at him. She looked so soft and small. He shifted her head so that it was in the nook between his shoulder cap and neck. He could look down at this sight for the rest of his life.

"I'm not interested in any man in town," she said. "I watched them all grow up. I remember when they ate boogers. How can I kiss someone who ate his own boogers?"

It was funny, but Brandon wasn't laughing. He was too focused on the implications of that statement. "You've never kissed anyone?"

Reegan's cheeks reddened. She didn't lift her head from his shoulder, but she did tilt her gaze down. "I didn't say that."

By the way she looked away from him, Brandon

got the feeling she hadn't. What was wrong with the men in this town? How could they resist the taste of the sweetness of her lips? They all were cracked in the head if they preferred boogers to Reegan Cartwright.

But he had to put that aside. He didn't want her thinking about other men. He definitely didn't want her thinking of California.

"But you'd rather stay here if you could?" he said.

She lifted her gaze back to his, and his breath caught. She was, without a doubt, the most beautiful woman he'd ever seen in his life. He would do anything to keep her close to him.

"I would," she said. "I love it here. I've never had any desire to leave. I'd miss the blooms. I'd miss my friends. I'd miss the choir."

All of a sudden, her words made complete sense to him. He couldn't see any reason for leaving this place either? Especially if he saw the blooms while standing at her side. He'd happily mix with her friends. He definitely wanted to hear her sing every day for the rest of his life.

"I mean, I could sing anywhere. But I love singing in that church surrounded by the people I've known all my life. It's all I've ever wanted to do. I'm afraid I don't have any other ambitions except to sing there. Sing solos, sing in a group, sing to myself."

"So stay."

"I will."

Reegan shifted her body until her forehead fit under his chin. Brandon's hold tightened around her.

"I'll stay for a while," she said. "But if the paperwork with my brother doesn't get sorted, I can't afford my own place. All my spare money went into home repair."

"So, stay here," he said.

Brandon's heart raced inside his chest. He was certain she could feel it. The organ was pounding so hard he was sure it knocked against her skull.

Reegan lifted her head and looked up at him, a question in her raised brows.

"Stay here with me." Brandon heard his mouth speaking. He didn't try to shut up. He agreed with every impulsive word he spoke. "You know how the Purple Heart Ranch works. Married soldiers get a house for their families, and then they can stay forever."

Reegan pushed away from him and sat up tall. Her lips parted as she regarded him. Had she stopped breathing as she waited for his next words?

Brandon knew he'd stopped breathing as he waited for her to say something, anything. But she just stared. And so he allowed what was in his heart to fill the silence.

"If we got married, you could have a home in your name. You'd be near the garden. You'd be near all of your friends. You wouldn't have to work a day in your life. And you could sing all you want."

Now that the words were out, he couldn't take them back. And the truth was, he didn't want to.

CHAPTER FOURTEEN

Reegan let the dark, rich soil sift through her fingers. Once it was all gathered in a pile, she patted the mound to secure the tall plant. Instead of climbing, the thin part at the top of the large stalk drooped.

Reaching for a stick and some thin rope, Reegan bound the wilting vine to the sturdy stick to help keep it straight as it grew. Now that it could reach the sun's rays, the plant would definitely grow and thrive.

She sat back and admired her handy work. Looking down at the plant, she felt a kindred spirit. Reegan had been planted in fertile soil. She'd been nurtured by her environment. But she'd never thrived, not truly. In the last few days, she'd been dealt tragedy after tragedy. She hadn't wilted because there was a strong post at her side.

Stay here with me.

Her heart lurched the moment the words had left his mouth. Reegan wanted to stay by Brandon's side forever. Unlike what Pastor Barrett had said, Brandon Lucas was not a stranger. Reegan felt she knew him better than any man of her entire acquaintance. Except, of course, for her brother.

Reegan had never had that type of reaction with any other man. Heck, she'd never truly kissed another man. Well, if she wanted to get technical, there had been Kenny Pratt, but he hadn't counted. Why? Because he'd missed her lips and tongued her nose; an unhappy event neither of them ever brought up again. It was also what solidified Reegan's belief that the boys of this town preferred boogers.

There had never been a man like Brandon Lucas in this town or in her life. Even now, she wanted to close her fingers around his. She wanted to rest her head against the strong beat of his heart. She wanted to stay inside the safety of his arms. The world could crash and burn while she was with him, and it wouldn't matter. It would hurt, but she'd be safe in his arms.

"How are you holding up?"

Reegan looked up to see Maggie Banks waddling up to her. The woman was near the second trimester of her pregnancy, and she looked like she was having twins. Two dogs trailed at her feet, her ever watchful army. Reegan was surprised she didn't see Dylan, Maggie's overprotective husband, in his wife's wake. But she supposed the dogs were protection enough.

"It's a bit of a lot," Reegan said in answer to Maggie's question.

The Irish Terrier, Spin, pulled up to a stop next to Reegan. The dog's hind legs hung limp in the wheelchair apparatus that Maggie had fashioned for him. Now, instead of being disabled, the dog was a holy terror. But his bright eyes and enthusiastic sniffs made everyone who came in contact with him fall instantly in love.

Spin rested his head on Reegan's lap and looked up at her with those doleful eyes. Reegan scratched the little dog's head and heard him sigh in utter contentment.

Maggie folded herself down into a crossed legged position in the dirt. Reegan worried the woman might not be able to make it back up again. But Sugar, her Golden Retriever, stayed at her side.

Once his mistress was seated, the large dog leaned into her back as though he were propping her up.

"You've been through more in the past week than anyone should have to manage in a lifetime," Maggie said.

Reegan took a deep breath, inhaling the crisp afternoon air. "I'm waiting for the lesson of it all."

Because there had to be a lesson, a silver lining. She knew her parents were in heaven and safe with God. She still wasn't convinced that her brother had met his glory. When her house had burned down, her faith had been shaken.

Reegan had been stripped of everything. Her family. Her possessions. Her belongings. But she had to believe it was all for a reason.

"You know you can stay here as long as you need," said Maggie. "We have plenty of room in our place."

"Brandon—Corporal Lucas—asked me to stay forever."

Maggie's brows rose. But not in alarm that a stranger had proposed a marriage of convenience to her. The soldier's wife's eyes shone bright with approval.

Reegan knew the story of Maggie and Dylan. Maggie had been a regular at the church since she was a girl. Though she'd never come with parents, always on her own. The veterinarian had had a tough beginning as a foster child, but she never lost faith. When Maggie had been kicked out of her apartment for having too many dogs, she'd walked right into a miracle. The miracle happened on this ranch where she met Dylan. They'd agreed to a marriage of convenience so he could stay on the ranch. In exchange, she could keep her dogs here and out of a pound where the disabled brood would've surely met their maker. In the course of events, after the wedding, the two fell madly in love.

That story had repeated four more times with the other soldiers who lived here on the Purple Heart Ranch. And it looked like the tradition would continue with Reegan and Brandon.

"Brandon asked me to marry him. You know, like you all did for the zoning."

The soldiers had thought the zoning regulations were a curse. But the rules had turned out to be a blessing in disguise as they'd each found the woman they'd spend the rest of their lives with. Maybe the same rules would now work in Reegan's favor?

"Oh, honey," Maggie beamed at her. But she shook her head at the same time, which confused Reegan. Those two words were cautionary, but she said them with joy. "They all say it's for the zoning; a marriage of convenience. It never is. It always winds up turning into lasting love."

Reegan's heart skipped at that thought. Her mouth became parched under the cloudy sky. Her fingertips itched as they sank into the rich soil.

"Is that what you want?" asked Maggie. "Do you have feelings for Corporal Lucas?"

"I barely know him."

Yet she'd spent last night in his bed with him by her side. In a chair. But it was still more intimate than she'd ever been with a man. And there was the way he'd held her that morning before he'd made his proposal. Reegan was certain she could stay in Brandon Lucas's arms forever.

"Eva and I barely knew Dylan and Fran before we said *I do*. And look at us."

That was true. It was all shaping up to be another purple-hearted love story. Except for one difference.

"Brandon feels guilty about what happened to Reece," Reegan admitted. "He even mentioned that he thinks the fire was partly his fault."

"Guilt is a powerful motivator," Maggie agreed. "But not enough to force a man into marriage. I've seen him looking at you these past few days.

Especially that first day when you were singing in church. He looked like he'd found heaven."

Reegan went breathless. A light wind sent a shiver over her skin raising goosebumps. Maggie reached out her hand, and Reegan took it, needing something to hold onto.

"Just be sure it's what you want," said Maggie.

Was it what she wanted? Reegan knew she wanted to sing. She knew she wanted to stay in her home town. She knew she wanted to be held in Brandon's arms. With this arrangement, she could spend forever doing all those things.

She had her answer.

CHAPTER FIFTEEN

The tap-tap-tapping sound was incessant, like the clatter of rounds firing and shell casings falling to the ground. Brandon couldn't stop his restless legs from moving. His entire body felt hot and cold at the same time. He needed somewhere for the energy to go.

He took a deep breath, closing his eyes. He knew before his lashes touched the tops of his cheeks that the move was a mistake. Heat flared behind his lids. Tingling started in his palms. The muscles in his chest tightened.

He saw smoke in his mind's eye. But he didn't see brown and orange hues of the desert. He saw the lush green and sturdy red brick of suburban America. The fire raged, and the brick of the house melted as he stood gaping in the street. Instead of a red-haired Reece, he saw the flames of Reegan's long tresses as she looked up at her home in horror.

Her gaze went wide as the explosion rocked the foundation of her home. The blast knocked her off her feet. Before Brandon could move, smoke sank low to the ground and engulfed her body. He tried to get to her, but his body wouldn't move. He was standing instead of lying face down, but it didn't matter. His feet wouldn't move. They were mired in something dark, thick, and black as night.

It was guilt.

Brandon's stomach churned. His breathing came in shallow pants until he roared. Brandon fought with everything in him, but the shame had a vise on him. As his internal battle raged, Reegan was swallowed whole by the gray cloud.

"Corporal Lucas?"

Brandon's eyes slammed open to find Dr. Patel standing a few feet away. Having dealt with PTSD issues, it was clear that the man knew to keep his distance until he was sure the way was safe. Brandon was no threat to anyone other than himself.

"I take it sleep is still eluding you?" The man took slow steps until he came behind his desk. His brown features were smooth and placid as he spoke. He leaned back in his chair, his hands folded on the top of his blank notepad.

Brandon sighed, trying to shake off the daydream. His head felt light after he pushed out the last of his heavy breaths. The tightening in his chest didn't lighten. But his leg tapping slowed a bit.

"When's the last time you slept?" Dr. Patel picked up his fountain pen. His scribbles filled the spaces were his taps had slowed.

Brandon thought back to the last time he'd slept longer than a few minutes. It had been the first night he was there. Right after hearing Reegan sing at church. He'd awakened feeling a peace he hadn't known in months. Just the thought of it made his toe-tapping slow down even more, but he hadn't come to a complete stop.

"It's been a couple of days," Brandon admitted.

Dr. Patel pulled his notepad onto his lap, blocking Brandon's view of his notes. "That would've been your first night here?"

Brandon nodded.

"After you came from the church?"

Brandon's gaze narrowed at the man. He watched as the pen moved across the paper, but there were no scritch scratch noises filling the silent beats between his foot tapping any longer.

"Reegan was lucky you were in the neighborhood the other night," Patel continued.

"Maybe. Maybe not."

Dr. Patel looked up. The pen went still as he regarded Brandon.

"Maybe I distracted her, and that's why the fire happened."

Dr. Patel sat the pen down on the desk. And then the notepad. As Brandon had suspected, there were hardly any marks on the lined paper.

Brandon had the sudden urge to fill that blank sheet of paper with his truth. And so he opened his mouth, and the guilt that had been clawing at him spilled out. "First, I took her brother from her, and now, I've taken her home from her."

Dr. Patel was silent for a long moment. He didn't reach for the pen and paper. He didn't downplay or deny Brandon's claims.

After another long, silent moment, Brandon frowned. Why wasn't the shrink telling him he wasn't at fault? Wasn't that his job? To assuage him of his guilt?

"I read the fire marshal's report," Dr. Patel finally said. "The report said the fire was due to faulty wires."

Brandon chewed at the inside of his lip. The

tightness in his chest moved up to his throat, closing off any words.

"I also read the military report on Private Cartwright's incident." Dr. Patel leaned forward, folding his forearms over the pad on the desk. The pen rolled off to the side. "You both followed protocol."

"I hesitated."

Dr. Patel steepled his fingers and rested his chin. His gaze was like iron as it held Brandon's. "Many a man has. Decisions are rarely black and white. There will always be shades of gray. It's the strong man that realizes that in a world of gradations, all he can do is what is right."

Brandon took a deep breath. He'd heard a Monday morning quarterbacking speech such as that before. It didn't change the fact that he couldn't stop wishing he'd made different decisions. If he hadn't let Cartwright go down and investigate, the man would still be alive. If he hadn't startled Reegan, she wouldn't have come to the front door, and her house wouldn't have burned down.

Dr. Patel shook his head slowly, as though he could hear Brandon's thoughts. "Until you let go of your guilt, you won't find peace or rest. That's why I wanted you to tend to something else. To work in the gardens, put the seeds in the soil, clear their paths, and watch the plants grow. But I see you found something else in the garden. News has spread of your proposal."

Brandon sat back in his chair, angling his body away from the doctor. Dylan and the others had joked that the man might be psychic. Brandon had never believed in unseen powers and reading people's minds, but now he wasn't so sure. "How did you find out?"

"Maggie."

So, it wasn't a psychic connection, just a gossiping pregnant woman. Reegan must have told her. Brandon had watched Maggie Banks waddling around the ranch. But apparently, she moved fast when she had a juicy tidbit to share.

"Pastor Barrett came to me," said Dr. Patel. "We are both pastors in the church. He wanted to know what kind of man you were."

"What did you tell him?" Suddenly Brandon's limbs and organs were still and silent. He cared very much what the two pastors thought of him.

Dr. Patel took a deep breath and picked up his pen again. "I told him that I'm not entirely sure your decision-making isn't impaired."

But hadn't he just said Brandon was blameless?

That he was a strong man and shades of gray and … what else had he said? Brandon couldn't remember the words from just a moment ago.

"You understand that lack of sleep leads to a myriad of impairments, one amongst them is poor impulse control and poor judgment?"

Brandon sat up stiff. "That had nothing to do with my relationship with Reegan. Proposing to her was a purely logical decision. She needs a home and a provider. She needs to be around those that care about her and not go to California. I can give those things to her if I marry her."

A broad smile spread across the doctor's face. He pushed the pen and the notepad off to the side of the desk. Brandon felt as though he'd passed some test he wasn't aware of taking.

"She would have a home," said Dr. Patel. "She'd also have a husband looking after her, tending to her. And she would look after and tend to you."

"Are you trying to say Reegan is my cure?"

Patel shrugged. But he did it with a smug smile. "I'm old fashioned, biblically old fashioned. Of faith, hope, and love; love is the greatest of the three. That's in Corinthians."

Brandon wasn't sure he had any of those three. He wasn't in love with Reegan. He didn't think?

But the thought of Reegan as his wife sent a shock of peace all through him. She would be his to provide for. His to protect. His to hold and keep safe. He wanted it more than a good night's sleep.

Maybe taking care of Reece's sister would assuage his guilt. Surely, that was more noble and useful than plucking weeds or talking about his feelings. Brandon was a man of action, a man who'd pledged his life to service and protection. More than anything, he wanted to serve and protect Reegan Cartwright. Not only because he loved looking at her, not only because he loved listening to her sing, but because he simply loved being around her.

Marriage had never been his plan. He'd had every intention of re-enlisting, of going back into service, and fighting for his country. But what if he found something else to fight for? What if he could stay on home turf and protect someone?

"You're a soldier to your core," Patel was saying, making Brandon think again about the man's psychic ability. "It's a different battle here. You have to decide what you're fighting for. And who."

CHAPTER SIXTEEN

"Aren't you going to stay?"

Reegan watched Brandon hesitate at her words. Oh, no. Had her voice been too needy? Was she being clingy?

They'd driven with Cassie and Xavier into town. The plan was for Brandon and Reegan to drive back in her truck which someone had brought from her house and to the church. So, it was entirely sensible that she ask him that question. He was her ride. She'd need to know where he was so they could ride back together.

Unless he hadn't planned to ride back with her. What if he'd planned to stay in town, see some of the nightlife? He was a soldier just off deployment. He'd been away for over a year. And even though he'd asked for her hand, he wasn't about to get his kicks with her.

Reegan was a modern woman but not that modern. She was considering marrying this man. She wasn't considering hopping into bed with him.

And maybe that's why he was thinking about heading out to sample some of the town's nightlife.

"You don't mind?" Brandon asked.

Just like that, all the tension left her shoulders. Gazing up into Brandon's eyes, she saw an eagerness there. He wanted to stay, but he was unsure if he was welcome.

"Of course not. I'd like it very much if you did. I want you to hear."

He smiled at her. Just a lift of the right corner of his mouth. But his eyes sparkled as he did so.

Reegan was lost. Her knees felt weak. Her heart fluttered like the butterflies flitting around the flowers she tended in the garden.

"I like hearing you sing," he said. "I love the sound of your voice."

"Oh? Well, that's good. Because I love to sing. I sing a lot."

"You won't hear any complaints out of me."

"Good."

Somehow, they were standing only an inch apart.

Somehow, his fingers brushed her forearm. Somehow, his gaze was fastened to her lips. Reegan wasn't sure if she wanted to sing for him or pull him in for a kiss?

"I'm so sorry for your loss."

At the sound of the feminine voice, Brandon pulled away from her. His face, so open a second before, shuttered like blinds being closed on a sunny day. Reegan turned to find Dakota Harris. The petite alto reached out her arms and folded Reegan inside.

For a moment, Reegan wasn't sure what was happening. And then she remembered. Reece. He was still missing, and everyone else thought him dead.

"We've taken up a donation for you," said Dakota. "Clothes and shoes and gift cards so you can replace other things."

Right. Her house had burned down. Reegan knew she should feel numb and devastated due to her losses. But she didn't. She felt blessed. She'd lost all her belongings, but her community was showering her with both material things and love.

"Thank you, Dakota," was all Reegan could manage.

Her brother was still MIA, but every day she

didn't get a call that the military had found his body, her hope and faith remained intact.

"It's awful that the insurance company won't hand you the check," said Noah Harris, one of the baritones in the choir. The man's gray mustache touched the bottom of his nose, causing him to wrinkle it.

Reegan wasn't complaining. She'd take not getting a check if there was a possibility that her brother was alive. Reece was strong. He was stubborn. She knew in her heart, that if he was able to, he'd come through and find a way home.

Now she had Brandon, a man who wanted to protect her, and provide for her, and hear her sing. In truth, she hadn't lost anything. Her cup runneth over.

Brandon had taken a seat in the back of the room, but Reegan felt his gaze on her from the moment she left him. His face was no longer open as it had been when they were standing close. It remained closed, but not his eyes. His eyes were filled with admiration as he watched her. The butterflies in her heart were working overtime.

Could it be possible that she was coming to have feelings for this man? She didn't need to question. She knew it was true.

No one had ever given her butterflies. No one had ever made her feel warm and safe. No one had ever looked at her as though she were both special and desirable. Because that was desire in Corporal Brandon Lucas's gaze. She wasn't so innocent that she didn't know what a man's hunger looked like.

As rehearsal began, Reegan's voice sailed from somewhere in the depths of her soul. Her every note was pitch perfect. Her voice lifted above everyone else's until all eyes were on her and all other voices went mute.

Gone was the cold and emptiness that had robbed her of her voice a few days ago. Gone was the heaviness on her shoulders and the hollow feeling in her heart. Reegan felt full. The feelings spilled out of her heart and drifted over her tongue.

All the while, she held Brandon's gaze. He watched her as though he were in rapture. At one point, his eyes closed as though he were in ecstasy... and they didn't open again until practice was over.

One by one, the other choristers filed out until it was just Reegan and Brandon left alone in the room. She came to him on quiet feet. She sat down next to him, the wood of the pew creaking as she did so. But still, he didn't stir.

She wasn't sure what to do. She'd never had to

awaken any man besides her brother. She tried calling his name quietly. But still, he dozed.

She laid a hand on his forearm. His skin was warm to the touch. The tiny hairs she found there tickled her fingertips.

Then her hand was snatched away from his arm. Her fingers wrenched. Brandon looked at her wild-eyed.

It took him a second before recognition dawned. And then his dark eyes filled with horror. His cheeks went beet red, and he groaned.

"Sorry," he said gruffly. "I wouldn't have hurt you."

"I don't doubt it."

She had been startled. But not frightened. She knew better than to come upon a soldier unaware. Her brother had warned her. But just as she felt no fear from Reece, she felt none from Brandon.

"Reegan, you can't ... you can't ..." There was so much shame, and guilt digging into the features of his face, making grooves and leaving frown marks.

"I'm sorry," she said. "I know better. You just looked so peaceful."

"I'm not." His gaze darkened. "There's a war raging in my mind."

"You have PTSD?"

The muscles in his neck worked. "It's not severe, like some others. But when I close my eyes, I see ..."

He was silent for so long. Reegan ached to reach out to him, to take him into her arms. And so she did.

She wrapped her arms around him and held him tight. He was stiff at first, but then he relaxed in her hold. His own grip became a vise around her.

"Listen, Reegan," he said into her hair. "About that thing I asked you—"

"That thing? You mean to marry you?"

"Yes."

She felt his breath at the cone of her ear. The single word was like a match. Her ear was the fire. The flame tunneled through her entire body. But then, it was doused by a single doubt.

"Are you taking it back?" she asked.

Reegan pulled back, but she didn't get far. Brandon's hold on her was absolute. She couldn't have gotten away if she'd tried. She did not try.

"No." His insistence was vehement.

Relief swam through her. The single word stoked the fire that had been lit a second ago. She felt the flames rising higher and higher.

"I just want you to know there's no rush," Brandon continued. "You've been through a lot. I don't want to add any pressure to you. The offer stands today, tomorrow, next week. However long you need. Whatever answer you want to give. I want you to know that I'll be here. For ... whatever you need."

Reegan's muscles relaxed as the heat between them worked its way through her limbs. "Brandon, you should know that my answer is yes."

"It is?" His voice, so hot and sure a moment ago, came out on a dry croak.

She nodded. They were holding each other in a loose embrace. She would swear that she felt the heat of him rise a few degrees under her fingertips.

"Well." He cleared his throat. "Good." He swallowed. "Fine. I suppose I'll let Dr. Patel and Dylan know so arrangements can be made."

"Brandon?"

"Yes, Reegan?"

"You can kiss me. If you want."

"I could?"

"Well, we are going to be married. So ..."

"That's true," he agreed. "Kissing is part of the ceremony. So, we should probably prepare for it."

"That's smart." Reegan pursed her lips, tugging them into her mouth to moisten them.

"They teach us to be prepared in the army."

"Sounds like good preparation."

Brandon took a deep breath. He leaned closer, pulling her body toward his. The bench squeaked again.

Reegan tilted her head up. She felt the warmth of Brandon's breath on her lower lip. It robbed her of the moisture she'd just licked into her lips. She didn't have time to prepare again. It was going to happen. Her first kiss. And not with some boy from around the block. It would be with a real man, a man who was going to be her husband very soon.

He was just an inch away now. Any second and she would—

The door to the room wrenched open. She saw Brandon's gaze slide away from his intended target, which had been her mouth, to scope out the intruder. Whomever he saw standing in the doorway must have been a threat because he pulled away from her.

Reegan looked up to find Pastor Barrett standing in the doorway. The older man glared at Brandon. Brandon stood to attention, leaving her alone on the bench. It looked like her first kiss would have to wait even longer.

CHAPTER SEVENTEEN

The sun was dipping down below the horizon when Brandon put Reegan's Ford F-150 in park outside their home.

Their home.

When had he switched over from thinking of the small row house as a borrowed home to claiming it as a homestead for him and his soon to be wife? Probably a second after she said yes to his proposal. He turned to her now, the last rays of the sun wrapped one of its tendrils around her cheek like a warm kiss.

Brandon wanted to take that trail. But he didn't. Not after the brief, but stern, chat they'd had with Pastor Barrett. It would seem that the senior pastor wasn't as enthused as Dr. Patel about their engagement.

The man had insisted on premarital counseling. Reegan had stepped forward. She'd agreed but on the condition that they receive their counseling from Pastor Patel and not the man who'd stepped into the role of father to her since her own father had passed away.

Pastor Barrett had clearly wanted to argue. But Reegan's jaw was set. Her chin was lifted high in defiance. Brandon hadn't necessarily wanted to spend hours each week under the man's disapproving glare, but he'd do it if that meant Reegan was the prize. Luckily, his bride to be was fierce, and the man of cloth acquiesced to her demands.

Now she sat comfortably in the passenger seat of her own vehicle, allowing Brandon to take the wheel. Something bloomed in Brandon's chest. He knew that he would protect this woman with everything in his heart. He would strive every day to ease her way in this life.

Reegan turned to him then, a small smile on her beautiful face. Brandon's breath caught. Though he still felt the claws of exhaustion right now, he pushed the feeling down. He didn't want to miss the opportunity to have his first taste of his soon to be wife. He'd been dreaming of brushing his lips against hers since ... well, since the first night he'd met her, and he'd fallen into the first contented sleep in months.

He parted his lips to take a deep breath, only to exhale a long yawn.

"Oh, are you tired?" asked Reegan.

"No, I'm not." Yes, he was. He hadn't gotten much sleep at all last night.

"I'm surprised after that nap you took during rehearsal."

"I'm sorry about that." He wrinkled his nose.

"I know some of the songs are boring and—"

"No, it wasn't that. It was your voice."

Her brows shot up in surprise. "My voice is boring?"

"No, no." Brandon took another deep breath. This time it came out on a sigh and not a yawn. "Your voice is beautiful, peaceful."

He searched for the words to make her understand the numbness he felt throughout the day. The incessant buzzing that ran through his head like a radio tuned to a defunct station.

"I told you it feels like a war raging in my mind," he said. "The constant noise and images keep me on high alert, keeps my adrenaline up. But when I hear you sing, it all just stops. And because it stops, I can rest."

She nodded, understanding clear in her blue eyes. "We can go inside and lay down." The moment the words left her lips her cheeks flushed a crimson red. "I didn't mean like that. I mean—I know we're getting married. And it's a marriage of convenience—"

Putting his arms around her waist, he pulled her to him, effectively hushing her errant thoughts. But also putting a point on the statement he was making. "I need you to understand that this marriage is more than a convenience for me."

"It is?" Her voice was breathless. Her eyes kept dipping down to his mouth.

Brandon had to swallow when she wet her lower lip. He was fascinated with everything that came out of her mouth. Including the small pink of her tongue. She could probably start quacking like a duck, and he'd be rapt with attention.

"Reegan, I wanted to kiss you since the first time I heard you open your mouth."

"Oh." She looked down. "Because my voice puts you to sleep."

He chuckled. With his other hand, he tilted up

her chin so that he could gaze directly in her eyes. His thumb brushed over her lower lip, giving himself a preview of what he was about to sample.

"Your voice gives me peace," he said. "Being with you gives me purpose. This marriage is more than about a home. Reegan, I want to give you the world."

"Oh," she sighed. Her warm breath brushed the tip of his thumb. "That's funny."

"Funny?"

"Maggie said it's never about the zoning."

It *was* about the zoning. Brandon wanted to mark Reegan Cartwright as his territory. In fact, that was exactly what he was going to do. There were no pastors around to stop him.

Her eyes fluttered closed as he leaned down. His bottom lip got the first taste as it brushed against her upper lip. Just that small hint was enough to knock him back on his heels. He wondered if he'd actually fallen down when he heard a knock behind him.

Brandon turned to look out the driver's side window. When he saw the man standing on two firm legs, he glared. Even the sight of his superior officer didn't wipe the murderous look off his face.

Chase raised his hands in surrender. Ortega, who stood behind him took a step back. Smart man.

"I need a word," said Chase through the closed window.

Unfortunately, Brandon could hear him clearly. "Right now? This actual second?"

"It's important." At least the man had the common decency to look apologetic.

Brandon let go of Reegan's chin and opened the car door.

Chase's eyes glanced over to Reegan. "In private."

Chase's smile was gentle toward Reegan. It was clear he didn't want to exclude her, but it must be army business that she couldn't know. Brandon circled around to the other side of the car and handed her out.

"I'll meet you inside," she said to Brandon.

She reached up on her tiptoes and kissed him on the cheek. It wasn't the first kiss he wanted with her, but it would hold him over until they were alone. He'd be sure and lock the front door behind him as soon as he was done with this private matter that couldn't wait.

"So, it looks like you're sticking around after all," said Ortega.

Brandon didn't respond. He watched Reegan as she entered the house. She'd turned the knob easily. The door hadn't been locked. No one seemed to lock doors here. Why would they with a ranch filled with veterans and soldiers? It was the safest place in the world, a place he would want to raise a family. A family he'd never truly even thought about. But now all he could think about was his marriage to Reegan and the life they'd have together.

"I got a phone call from the DOD about the mission," said Chase. "They found something."

That snapped Brandon back to attention. "Reece? They found his body?"

"Not exactly. They're not sure. An informant came through with credible information. They had his tags."

"So, they want to ransom the body?" Bile filled Brandon's throat at the thought.

"No," said Chase. "They said he's alive."

Brandon went entirely still. Everything in him went still as well. The constant buzzing sounds went on mute. The flickering images that flashed through his mind on a constant reel went dark.

"The information is still classified," Chase continued. "I sent Reegan away because I didn't want to get her hopes up, not after everything she's been through. Our orders are to wait until it's been confirmed."

CHAPTER EIGHTEEN

"Have you set a date yet?"

Reegan sat two glasses of lemonade down on the kitchen table. Sarai wrapped perfectly manicured fingers around the tall glass and sipped carefully. Reegan knew the woman still struggled with an eating disorder and was very mindful of what she put in her body, which was why Reegan had gone light on the sugar.

Meanwhile, Eva DeMonti tossed her head back and tilted the yellow liquid until it was bottom's up. The co-ed then slammed the glass down for another, which Reegan happily refilled. Eva was constantly on the go between attending classes, wrangling her two tween siblings, and a husband who was also a busy body.

The two women had been walking by as Reegan had come out onto her front porch that morning. Reegan liked the sound of that; *her* front porch. She'd had an entire deck on her parents' house. And though it had been her home all her life, this small house that she'd only spent two nights in suddenly felt like her entire world.

Last night, Brandon had come inside. His features looked weary and tight. Reegan guessed that whatever private matter had been discussed between him and his fellow soldiers had weighed down on him. She decided not to press him on it. They were still getting to know each other, coming to trust one another with their secrets.

Brandon had walked her to his bedroom door. But after he'd ushered her inside, he'd stayed at the threshold. He insisted she take the larger room while he went off to the spare. Before Reegan could protest, he'd shut the door and was gone.

He'd also been gone early this morning before she'd awakened. She knew he hadn't gotten much sleep. She'd heard him tossing and turning and then up and about all night.

Something was wrong. When she saw him later, she was determined to get him to open up to her. She knew he probably couldn't tell her the details of the matter if it was army related. Reece had often had a heavy expression on his features when he was home on leave. Despite her insistence, he explained he couldn't give her all the details on his missions.

Reegan didn't need the details now. She just needed Brandon to know that she was there for him. She'd be happy if he rested his head in her lap while she sang to him.

"I bet the wedding will probably happen as quickly as this weekend," Eva was saying.

That snapped Reegan back to the present. Married? This weekend?

But just as much as the thought stole her breath, it created an equal ache in her heart. She didn't want to wait. She wanted to be Mrs. Brandon Lucas as soon as she could. She wanted to be his wife, and she wanted to make this house a home.

There was nothing in this place that was hers, not even the clothing she wore. It was all gifts and donations. Neither was there much in there that belonged to Brandon. The two of them would get to paint this blank slate together and make it theirs.

Again, her heart filled with so much joy of how blessed she was even in the light of all the tragedy she'd experienced. There had been a reason for it all. There had been a masterplan that brought her to this moment.

From deciding to stay and take care of the house left to her brother, to getting up and singing in the choir at that particular service. She'd been there at the right moment when Brandon had shown up. True, he'd come to tell her that her brother was missing, but her faith was still firm that Reece was with her if not in body then in spirit.

It had all led her to this moment, standing in her very own kitchen, preparing to marry the man of her dreams. Her singing had pierced Brandon's heart. If she hadn't have raised her voice, Brandon wouldn't have heard her sing. And now they'd be spending the rest of their lives together.

Reegan doubted they'd spend forever in this house on the ranch. But it would be a good start for them. There were two bedrooms, one for them and one for their first child. She hadn't even had her first real kiss yet, and she was already thinking about, well, more.

"Brandon and Reegan don't have to rush like we did," Sarai was saying.

"None of us had to rush," said Eva. "They all had months before that zoning about this land being for families only kicked in. Every one of them married before time was up."

"She's right." Sarai turned back to Reegan. "You'll likely be hitched by the weekend."

That sounded perfectly fine to Reegan. The sooner, the better.

"And then you won't be alone when he gets deployed again," said Eva. "You'll have us."

It took Reegan running the woman's words in her head over and over again to comprehend. Each time she replayed Eva's words her blood grew colder and colder until the pitcher of lemonade slipped out of her hands.

"When he what?" Reegan breathed, her voice barely above a whisper.

Eva and Sarai looked to each other. Concern was etched on both their honey-golden skin.

"I ..." Eva looked between Sarai and Reegan. "That's what he said his first night here."

"Brandon's deploying?" Reegan tested out the words. They tasted bitter on her tongue. "He's going back to war?"

"I could be wrong?" Eva's words rushed out. "That was his first day here before he met you."

"He met me before he came here."

"But he wasn't in love with you then," Sarai

offered. "He is now."

The back door opened. All three women turned to the large figure standing in the doorway. Brandon's gaze swept over the scene at the kitchen table. His eyes were bright, hungry as they searched for her. But the light dimmed when he saw her. The two other women quickly excused themselves.

Reegan couldn't look at him. Instead, she grabbed a rag and began mopping up the spilled lemonade. As she squeezed the sugary beverage from the rag, she felt all the joy squeeze from her heart.

"What happened?" Brandon asked.

"What does it look like?" she snapped, her voice breaking.

"I see the obvious answer is that someone spilled lemonade. But I don't think it's the right answer." He bent down and took the rag from her, finishing cleaning up the mess she'd made.

Reegan watched him. She watched how the muscles of his arms moved as he dragged the rag over the floor. She watched how his lips pursed in concentration of the job. She looked at the dark bags under his eyes and ached to soothe him, even now.

"When were you going to tell me?" she said.

He frowned, looking up at her. She saw her own

anguish reflected back at her from his dark eyes. His gaze turned guilty, and he turned away.

Brandon stood, tossing the rag into the sink and then washing his hands. He pumped soap into his palm and rubbed his hands together. Then he repeated the action as though he hadn't gotten clean enough the first time.

"So it's true?" Reegan asked coming to her feet. "You're re-enlisting and looking to deploy?"

"What?" Brandon whirled around to face her. "No. I'm not re-enlisting."

Reegan's relief was instant. So, it had been a misunderstanding? He wasn't leaving her. But then his gaze clouded over as he appeared to think about it more.

"Well, yes," he revised his answer. "I was. That was the plan. But then I met you and … everything changed."

Brandon opened his arms, and like she was a moth to his flame, she came to him. Her legs were shaky, and he caught her before she took the last step to bring them together. He wrapped her up in his warm embrace, and Reegan knew heaven.

"I have no idea what I'm going to do with my life now," he said into her hair. "Except for the fact that I want to spend it with you."

Reegan's whole being was a tornado of emotion. Everything was topsy turvy. Nothing was clear. She needed some clarity, something to hold onto. "So, you're not leaving?"

"No." He pulled away from her, gazing down into her eyes so that she saw the truth there. "I'm not leaving you."

The tears fell then. Reegan felt as though she'd been holding herself together, not just for days, but since her parents died. For his part, Brandon held her, he held her tight, whispering sweet-nothings in her ear.

She wasn't sure how they ended up in the bed. But his arms were around her. She felt his warm embrace even through the layers of clothing that remained between them. His large, strong body was a spoon behind her while she cried. He held her tight as though protecting her from all sides.

And cry she did, for hours, maybe even days, as she finally felt the effects of her world crashing down around her. But through it all, she knew she was safe. Nothing would ever hurt her again. Not while Brandon Lucas held her in his arms.

And hold her he did. He didn't loosen his grip for one second. Not when her tears stopped. Not when she fell asleep.

CHAPTER NINETEEN

It was the bright rays of dawn that awakened him. Not the whirring of a helicopter. Not the crunch of boots. Not the snore of someone sleeping next to him. Though someone was sleeping in his arms.

Reegan's back was tucked against his chest. They were both still fully clothed. His arms were wrapped firmly around her, holding her close. Against his forearm, he felt her chest rise and fall in the peace of sleep. Her fingers were entwined in his.

The last thing Brandon remembered was lying down with her in his arms as she cried herself to sleep. She'd finally reached the next level in her stage of grief. All because she'd thought he was preparing to leave her.

His hold on her tightened at the thought. He doubted he'd ever be able to be away from her for more than a few hours. In fact, in the bright morning light, even one hour felt excessive.

Brandon knew he'd carried Reegan in here when the sun was still high in the sky. Looking at the clock on the side table, he saw that it was the start of a new day. He didn't remember seeing the darkness of night.

Had he slept through an entire day? She hadn't even sung him to sleep. Her wails had pulled at his heart. He knew he hadn't closed his eyes until she'd settled. It must have been the act of holding her, of having her near that had brought him to the place of peace.

He had to have gotten at least ten hours of sleep, likely more. He hadn't wakened once in the night. Not even from a nightmare.

It wasn't her singing that gave him peace, it was her. He'd found hope in her. He'd found faith in her. He'd found love in her.

That young pastor was right; it wasn't good for man to be alone. Just as soldiers formed teams and units, Brandon had found his true calling with the woman in his arms. Holding the woman he would marry, he felt the chords of harmony settle over him.

Pressing the palms of their entwined fingers together, he found an unbreakable unity.

For the first time in a long time, Brandon wanted to sink to his knees and say thank you.

Later.

Right now, he pulled the woman who completed his life to him. He pressed his lips to her temple. Reegan stirred, turning her face to him and slowly blinking open her bright blue eyes.

Recognition was swift in her gaze. The smile she gave him lent him the strength of a full army. Her sigh of utter contentment, had he not been laying down, would've knocked him to his knees.

"Good morning," she said.

"Good morning," he parroted.

"I don't think we were supposed to sleep together until after the wedding."

She turned her body to face him. Brandon loosened his hold only slightly. He had no intention of letting her go right now or ever. Moving his fingertips through her mussed hair, he brushed her strands aside so that he could have a clear view down into her lovely face.

Brandon had never expected to fall in love. He was glad he was lying down for the occasion. It was a dizzying event.

Reegan looked up at him with so much trust in her eyes. But there was still a vulnerability on her brow. He wanted to brush it away. Before he could have that right, he'd need to come clean about everything.

"I blamed myself for your brother's ..." He couldn't use the word death now, since it may no longer be accurate. "For losing Reece. He asked permission to investigate something that seemed off. There were a group of women headed into a danger zone we were surveilling. He wanted to warn them. I thought they might be setting a trap. He argued against it. I let him convince me to take the chance."

Brandon took a breath. He waited for the darkness to assault him, for the smoke to fill his nostrils. The sights, sounds, and smells were all there, but they weren't strong. They were no longer a visceral experience, just a memory.

"Were they the bad guys?" asked Reegan.

"We still don't know for sure," Brandon answered. "But some evidence has come to light that we may have been wrong."

"Well, you could always count on Reece to do the right thing. Even if that meant he'd sacrifice himself for the possibility of the good in others. If he is gone, then I'm glad he did it trying to save someone else's life. And his last act brought you to me."

Brandon closed his eyes. There were no flames, no smoke, no sand behind his eyes. There was only the glow of orange-red. He'd rested his forehead against Reegan's forehead, and her hair filled his vision.

She was a blessing come to life. He felt he could breathe again. He felt absolved.

He opened his eyes in time to catch Reegan tilting her head. Both of her soft pink lips closed around his bottom lip. Brandon relaxed into her sweetness. One of his hands came up and cupped the side of her face, tilting her head so that he could capture both of her lips with his.

As much as he wanted to hear her voice, to hear the sweet songs she made, he wanted the sweetness of her lips even more. His fingers tangled in her hair, holding her to him, and he deepened the kiss.

Reegan gasped. The sound of her voice, coupled with the sweetness of her lips, added onto the softness of her flesh broke something inside Brandon. The soldier in him threw up his hands in surrender.

Before he could wave the white flag, a pounding knock sounded at the front door.

They both groaned. Neither pulled away from the other. Reegan's hunger for him was reflected in her blue gaze.

Just as Brandon thought to ignore it, the knock sounded again. He knew it wasn't one of the women from the ranch. It was an authoritative knock. Like a soldier's knock. But he knew it wasn't one of the men on the ranch.

Rolling out of bed, he ran his hand through his hair as he left the bedroom. He took a few deep breaths as he approached the door so that he wouldn't bite off the head of the person on his doorstep. Throwing open the wood door, Brandon's suspicions were confirmed. Standing on the stoop were two uniformed officers. Alongside them was Chase.

"Corporal Lucas?" said one of the uniforms.

Brandon nodded. He glanced over at Chase whose look was grim. Brandon's first thought was to shield Reegan from whatever news they were about to deliver. But it was too late. He already felt her coming up behind him.

"We have communication that Private Reece Cartwright has been found."

Reegan gasped behind him. Brandon turned with his arms outstretched in case she was about to faint. But who was he kidding? This was Reegan. The woman had been thrown tragedy after obstacle, and she was still standing.

Her blue eyes were bright. Her lips tilted up in a smug smile. "I told you."

Yes. She had told him. He knew now never to doubt his future wife's intuition.

"We're putting together a team to retrieve him," the uniformed soldier continued. "We'd like you to be on it."

CHAPTER TWENTY

Reegan's emotions were being tugged in two different directions. On the one hand, she'd been right. Her brother was alive. Her heart felt like it was expanding, growing ten times as large as though it could hoist a sail and head overseas to retrieve her brother. And that's where the tug in the other direction came into play.

She turned to Brandon. His jaw was tense. His hands were balled into fists.

In order to get her brother back, she'd have to relinquish her hold on the man she loved. She'd lost so much in the last week. Could she take the gamble and possibly lose more? There truly would be nothing left if they didn't recover Reece and Brandon didn't return.

Her heart, so heavy from the joyful news of her brother, broke into pieces of shard at the thought of losing the love of her life. Her insides felt sliced up at the two directions she was pulled. She wanted her brother back safe, but she didn't want to let go of Brandon.

Her fingers found his. Slowly he unballed his fingers and clutched her hand in his.

"Is this the only way?" she asked the two uniform soldiers sitting on their couch. Sergeant Chase stood near a window looking out at the ranch. Reegan sat in a wingback chair with Brandon standing over her like some great, protective beast.

"No," Brandon answered. "I don't have to be the one to go."

She'd only known this man for a handful of days, but she heard it clearly in his tone. He was not the type of man to push his responsibilities off on others. To shun this duty would take something from him. That something was a major part of what had made Reegan fall in love with him so fast and so surely.

She gave his hand a tug until he met her gaze. The turmoil in his dark eyes told her she had gotten it right. He wanted to go, but he didn't want to leave her.

"Corporal Lucas knows the terrain and the logistics," said the uniformed soldier. "He's the best man for the job on such short notice. Sgt. Chase said so."

Chase pushed off the wall and came closer. "I assumed you meant to consult him. I didn't realize you wanted him to go back."

"He's our best chance at getting Private Cartwright back," said the soldier.

"Which is why he's going."

All eyes came to Reegan. But she only had eyes for Brandon. She stood, turning her back and shutting the others out. She placed her hands on his heart and looked up into the face she'd come to cherish.

His gaze narrowed as he peered into her eyes. Words were not necessary between them. Reegan understood this man perfectly. And now she was certain he understood her.

"I have to do this," he said. "I have to go and bring him back."

"I know."

She reached out to bring him into her arms and found herself swallowed up in his embrace. She felt his deep and shuddery inhale. His exhale blew strands of her hair away and caressed the cone of her ear.

Reegan rested her head under his chin. She'd had so much taken away from her, but this was the one thing she wanted to hold onto; the safe place just above Brandon's heart.

She straightened, looking him in his beautiful eyes. Eyes that knew her so well after such a short time. She felt bared to this man.

They were alone now. At some point during their embrace and intimate conversation, the uniformed soldiers and Chase had left. But she could see them waiting outside the front door. It let her know that her time with Brandon was short. The clock was ticking before he'd leave.

Brandon put his forefinger under her chin and turned her attention back to him. "I need you to do something for me before I go," he said.

"Anything."

"Marry me."

Her breath caught at the fierceness in his strong features. She lifted a hand and ran it down the side of that strong jaw. "I already agreed to do that."

"I want to give you my vow before I go." His dark eyes practically glowed with emotion. His hold on her was firm. If she'd wanted to get away, it would've been an impossibility. "Not because I want you to have everything I own before I go. Because I need you to know that you have my heart, you have my strength, you have everything that I have to offer. Reegan Cartwright, you came upon me like a sneak attack, and you broke down all my defenses. I surrender to you."

She rested her forehead against his. He wiped the tears as they fell to her cheek. "We're lucky these guys and girls on the ranch know how to throw together a quickie wedding. Let's do it so you can bring me back my brother."

CHAPTER TWENTY-ONE

*B*randon opened his eyes. He blinked a few times and then he was wide awake. Sleep came to him with ease now that his spirit had found peace.

Nightmares still touched his dreams, but their grip was weaker. Dark thoughts flitted through his mind throughout the day, but he was overwhelmed by the bright blessings now present in his life.

He reached out across the mattress for the source of that wondrous warmth, but the space next to him was empty. It had only been two days since he'd slept with Reegan in his arms. The following two nights had been peaceful as he listened to her sing in their kitchen, as he listened to her hum in the gardens as they tended the soil side by side. She hadn't been in his bed again, but his body knew that her place was next to him.

Soon ...

The night after the soldiers had made their visit had been a whirlwind of preparation for both his mission as well as his wedding. The women of the Purple Heart Ranch had whisked his fiancée away, and he hadn't seen her again until dinner. They'd whisked her away again for the night for an impromptu bachelorette party.

The next day, he'd had some time with Reegan in the gardens. But as the following day would be their wedding day, tradition dictated that they spend the night apart.

Brandon found he slept each night peacefully even knowing the dangerous mission he was about to undertake. His mind was rested, and his soul was at peace. Be it because he had a chance to save Reece or because he had given his heart over to Reegan, he wasn't sure? Likely a bit of both.

So, it was easy to roll out of bed each morning and greet the day with less weight on his shoulders. He pulled on his uniform and stared at his reflection. For so many years his self-worth had been wrapped up only in how he could serve his country, the livelihood of his unit, and his personal performance. It had never occurred to him to serve one person above others, to stick to one community, to evaluate himself on his relationship to others. But that would be his life moving forward.

"Ready?"

Brandon looked up to Chase and Ortega standing in the door to his home. Like him, the men were decked out in their uniforms.

"Man," said Ortega. "Who would have thought that when we came here for a little R&R it would lead to a wedding. In just a week."

"Dylan warned us," said Brandon. "You two should be on the lookout."

Ortega snorted. "Yeah, no. I'm pretty sure we're good."

The two single men raised their fists and tapped their knuckles. Brandon got the sense that those were famous last words.

The three men walked out of the front door and down to the pavilion near the small body of water in the center of the ranch. A white gazebo trimmed with vines and flowers was the focal point. The rows of white chairs spread out before the gazebo were filled with a few rows of standing individuals.

It appeared the entire community had gathered for the wedding. Brandon recognized the soldiers from the ranch and their wives seated in the front. He also saw some familiar faces from the church choir.

"Thank you for your service," a kid said. The words were said with a lisp as the little boy was missing two front teeth.

Brandon reached down and gave the kid's head a pat. He heard the sentiment a few more times as he made his way to the gazebo where his nuptials would take place. Instead of getting annoyed at the sentiment, his heart swelled at the gratitude displayed.

He had served his country well. He was proud of that service. Now he would serve this community. Starting with taking care of their favorite daughter.

Music started to play from a speaker, and he saw her. Brandon's heart stopped for a few beats as she walked toward him. She was a vision in white, but more importantly, she was his.

Reegan walked on the arm of Pastor Barrett. The man glared at Brandon as he came closer. Brandon stood with his back even straighter. He met the man's glare with wide eyes and an open heart. If the pastor didn't see that he would do everything in his power to cherish the woman coming toward him, then Brandon would spend the rest of his life showing it to the man of the cloth. He'd spend his life showing it to everyone in this town that he was the best man for Reegan.

At the end of the aisle, Pastor Barrett turned to Reegan. She beamed up at the man who was a second father. His stern expression broke. It softened into love and adoration. A small smile remained in place when he turned to Brandon and presented him with his bride.

Brandon nodded his thanks. He stuck out his hand. Pastor Barrett's grip was strong. It also felt sure.

Turning his attention to Reegan, Brandon felt a little unsteady on his feet. She looked up at him with such trust, such certainty, such love. How had he come to deserve her?

A light wind brought the scent of honeyed flowers from the gardens. Mixed with that was the hint of hay from the barns. He hadn't believed in anything magical before setting foot on this ranch. Now he was a believer that there was something special about this place.

Love was in the rich soil underfoot. It blossomed for those who came here. Chase and Ortega didn't stand a chance if they planned to stay here for any length of time.

Brandon tucked Reegan's hand in the crook of his elbow and turned them to face Dr. Patel. The delight in the doctor's features eclipsed that of any other attendee. The knowing glint in his eyes made Brandon wonder if the man had foreseen this scene playing out.

After all, it had been Patel who'd sent him to the gardens instead of horseback riding. The man hadn't even blinked when, just days later, Brandon had proposed marriage to the woman who'd been tending the soil on that same day.

"Before we begin," said Dr. Patel, "Corporal Lucas has prepared some words."

Brandon cleared his throat. Turning to face Reegan, he took both her hands in his. Once again, her beauty and trust shook something inside until his knees quivered, but he did not hesitate, he did not falter.

"There's so much we don't know about each other, but I'm excited for the rest of my life. What I do know is that you're loyal and fierce. You feel deeply. So deeply that you've reached inside and forged a connection. I feel it. It's beyond my heart. It's in my soul. Though we're about to be parted for some time, I understand that you are a part of me, and I'm a part of you."

It took a few moments for the gathered crowd to settle. Sobs and moans went up. Tissues were passed around. And all the while, Brandon gazed into Reegan's eyes seeing the same certainty that he felt in his blood.

He meant every word, and he would prove it with actions. After years of fighting, peace settled over Brandon. Once the official vows were said by the two of them, he bent down and sealed his promise with a kiss. He embraced this new duty where he was ready, willing, and able to serve for his lifetime.

His eyes wrenched open. Though he was surrounded by gray and black shadows, he winced. A dull ache spread through his limbs now that he was conscious. His mouth was dry, and his mind was a swirling vortex of darkness.

He heard a voice next to him. Looking up, he saw someone whose face was covered in dark cloth. Only her eyes were visible. He knew it was a woman because of the length of her lashes, the kohl around her eyelids, and the soft lilt of her words.

He knew that she was no threat. Her words were hushed but not urgent. They were gentle but urging him into action. The words were also said on a foreign tongue. The sounds jumbled in his mind, but a second later, he understood them.

"What is your name?"

Four words. He understood their meaning, but he didn't know the answer.

What was his name? He knew he had one. It was there, somewhere in his brain. He just needed a light to shine in the darkness.

When a shard of brightness from somewhere in the room met his gaze, he instantly shut his eyes. It was too late, a vision slipped through. His entire body shuddered at a pain that wasn't his own. No, he would not go towards that light. Any illumination would only bring pain.

But he couldn't keep his eyes closed forever. Especially since the voice asking him questions was growing louder, more insistent. And so he peeked out from under his lashes.

The woman held up an object. It was a bound book. Somehow he knew it belonged to him, and he reached for it.

It was small, brown, and leather bound. There were burn marks at the edges, and a few of the pages were charred. *Daily Devotional Bible* was written in gold letters on the front face.

With ginger fingers, he opened the book. A folded piece of paper fell out. The corners flapped like a bird's wings bringing it in for a landing.

His eyes scanned over the writing. He knew that writing. It was the first familiar thing. He picked out a few words.

Love you.

Always.

Marriage.

Beth.

Beth? He felt possessive over that name. It wasn't his. Beth was a woman. Was she his woman?

I will always love you, Reece. If there's a chance ... marriage ... always yours ... Beth.

A feeling of serenity came over him. He wanted to be Reece. He wanted to have Beth's love. He just wished he could remember who she was. He wished he could remember who he was.

*You won't want to miss the reunion
between Reece and Beth.*

*Watch as true love is realized in
Always On My Mind
the seventh book in The Brides of Purple Heart Ranch!*

Shanae Johnson was raised by Saturday Morning cartoons and After School Specials. She still doesn't understand why there isn't a life lesson that ties the issues of the day together just before bedtime. While she's still waiting for the meaning of it all, she writes stories to try and figure it all out. Her books are wholesome and sweet, but her are heroes are hot and heroines are full of sass!

And by the way, the E elongates the A. So it's pronounced Shan-aaaaaaaa. Perfect for a hero to call out across the moors, or up to a balcony, or to blare outside her window on a boombox. If you hear him calling her name, please send him her way!

You can sign up for Shanae's Reader Group at http://bit.ly/ShanaeJohnsonReaders

Also By Shanae Johnson

The Brides of Purple Heart

On His Bended Knee

Hand Over His Heart

Offering His Arm

His Permanent Scar

Having His Back

In Over His Head

Always On His Mind

Every Step He Takes

In His Good Hands

Light Up His Life

Strength to Stand

The Rangers of Purple Heart

The Rancher takes his Convenient Bride

The Rancher takes his Best Friend's Sister

The Rancher takes his Runaway Bride

The Rancher takes his Star Crossed Love

The Rancher takes his Love at First Sight

The Rancher takes his Last Chance at Love

The Rebel Royals series

The King and the Kindergarten Teacher

The Prince and the Pie Maker

The Duke and the DJ

The Marquis and the Magician's Assistant

The Princess and the Principal